UnAmerica

UnAmerica
Momus
Success and Failure Series
Catalogue No. PA-017

First published in the United States of America in 2014
by Penny-Ante Editions, *penny-ante.net*

LIBRARY OF CONGRESS CATALOGING-IN-PUBLICATION DATA
Momus, 1960-
  Unamerica / Momus. — 1st ed.
    p. cm.
ISBN 978-0-9855085-9-3
  1. Fiction—General. 2. Fiction—Literary.

Printed in the United States of America.
Distributed in the United States of America by SCB Distributors.
Distributed in the United Kingdom by Turnaround Publisher Services.

PENNY-ANTE | EDITIONS
PO BOX 691578 LOS ANGELES CA 90069
UNITED STATES OF AMERICA

Other Works by Momus

The Book of Jokes
DALKEY ARCHIVE PRESS

The Book of Scotlands
STERNBERG PRESS

The Book of Japans
STERNBERG PRESS

UnAmerica
Momus

Penny-Ante Editions
Success and Failure Series

1

It's a sunny afternoon during the month of Hekatombaion. Wild pear trees—glabrous, their leaves cordate, nearly orbicular, their nuts oval—are coming into flower. I'm headed eastbound on Tupperway Drive. I make an illegal U-turn at the Boone Hill United Methodist Church and am soon pulling my Dodge Custer into the Tastee Freez car park.

Inside the restaurant, I'm ushered to a booth where I order a Hot Fudge Sundae with a large side of fries.

This is not the sort of food I normally eat, or even like very much, to be honest. I prefer to picnic alone in the middle of a field somewhere, with a pot of raspberry jam, two slices of crisp bread, a hard-boiled egg, and some unsugared tea in a Thermos flask.

The wind might rustle in the willows, rabbits might graze in the boskiness of a hedgerow, and John Constable would probably be standing at an easel nearby, whistling as he smears flecks of Cremnitz white from a soft metal tube into a lowering and turbulent paint sky.

After lunch I will push my bicycle over the recently-ploughed sod, casting a lustful yet repressed eye at a handsome farm labourer stripped to the waist, and cycle to the nearest village, where I will seek out junk shops selling bric-a-brac, or perhaps stumble on a serendipitous church fete.

"Brad?"

The frail, fussy voice takes me by surprise; an old man dressed like a janitor emerges from a utilities closet.

"Brad, thank you for coming. I know that many people would assume this was a hoax. You have shown yourself to be a true believer."

"Uh, great to meet you!"

God's handshake isn't particularly firm. His foreign accent, darting brown eyes, swarthy complexion and cheap nylon janitor's uniform make him look like an illegal kitchen worker from the Middle East.

"Now Brad", says God, "you're going to have to make allowances for me. I have late-onset Alzheimer's disease."

"I'm very sorry to hear that!"

"Yes, it's my cross to bear, so to speak. I've totally forgotten how to create things. Do you know what my main project is right now, Brad?"

"I wouldn't presume to guess or know, sir!"

"I want to uninvent America, a nation I have come to despise."

This is surprising.

"Why do you despise America?"

God knits his brows.

"Because Americans have lost touch with everything important.

They've become fat, greedy, selfish pigs."

God explains how little he was impressed by the mass extermination of indigenous peoples, the triumph of the slave-driving South over the Yankees during the Civil War, and the Confederate States of America's use of nuclear weapons against civilian populations in Britain during the Second World War.

"That sounds fair enough", I observe. "I'm a secret British sympathiser myself."

My sundae and fries arrive. God is talking about the Hutterites; how they were the only Americans to have followed his injunction in the Acts of the Apostles to pool their possessions, sell all their goods and distribute them according to need.

"And you know what they got for this, Brad? They were called communists, jailed, beaten up, killed. The states started passing laws forbidding them to buy more land. They had to move to Canada.

"Brad, Americans have become the opposite of everything I intended humans, and especially Christians, to become. If I still could, I'd smash this nation to potsherds, or flood the entire continental basin from sea to shining sea."

God becomes suddenly businesslike.

"I am seeking a faithful servant to recreate in reverse the voyage of Saint Brendan, dearly beloved to me. Do you know much about him?"

Nibbling on a french fry, I confess that I don't know anything about Saint Brendan.

God explains that the monk set off from Ireland in the early

6th century, inspired by a holy man called Mernoke, who had discovered a magical land beyond the western horizon where every herb was full of blossom and every tree full of fruit. This, says God, was Eden, or Tir na nÓg, the earthly paradise where death and disease were unknown. Brendan set off in a coracle with twelve hand-picked associates, hoping to discover this land. After seven years of paddling from island to island, he succeeded.

God shakes some hundreds-and-thousands onto the surface of my fudge sundae. Calm, epic music punctuated by the cries of sea birds fills the air. We crane over the glass and seem to be zooming in on a tiny boat crossing an ocean of whipped cream.

"The Irish discovered America", says God. "But the earthly paradise has become an unparadise. The whole situation has to be reversed. America has to be undiscovered. People need to turn their backs on all it stands for. People need to learn about—and learn from—the rest of the world.

"Now it's the rest of the world that needs to become the shining example, the Tir na nÓg, the Shangri-La, the Golden Fleece.

"You, Brad, and your twelve hand-picked companions must learn—and teach the world—how to become as unAmerican as possible. That is my final wish, and my last command. Do you accept the challenge?"

What can I say?

2

My first memories are of Bangkok. I was born there. My father was teaching Archeology at Thammasat University. He drove a cream-coloured Mercedes 230 SL convertible with diplomatic plates. My mother was so busy whirling through Bangkok society in Pucci prints and Marimekko dots that she quite neglected me and my sister Gertli. We were raised by rounded, kindly Thai servants.

At the age of five—just before visiting the Confederate States of America for the first time—I fell in love with a mafoo, a Chinese stable boy of epicene, semi-equine beauty. The mafoo, who worked at a riding school run by Cossacks, wore a dark shirt lined with white butchers' stripes, and over it a small waistcoat of felt. His trousers were both baggy and tightly tapered. On his head tottered an enormous conical hat, secured under the neck with a strap.

Aside from being a hedonist and a dandy, my mother was a Christian Scientist. The servants had strict instructions not to treat us with any medications should we fall ill. As a result, my whole childhood seemed to pass in a fever. I believed very devoutly in God, and would lie in bed for hours talking to him.

There's so much more I should have asked God at our meeting. How would things have turned out if the North had won the Civil War and slavery had been abolished? How do I soften oak bark with butter when tanning the hides that will form the leather underbelly of my coracle? What criteria should I use when picking my twelve associates? Should I tell potential recruits the true purpose of the mission?

I decide that would be dangerous; anything anti-American passes for terrorism. It'll be far more effective to present the mission as a rugged marine adventure like *Deadliest Catch*, the Discovery Channel's series about fishing for king crab in Alaska. Untrammelled masculinity is something most American males can get behind. Most American females too.

I need to hang out someplace that attracts men who love ocean adventure. When I get home I hit the Salt Life Apparel website and call up a page entitled "The Salt Life Story".

"The four partners of Salt Life are avid watermen and extreme surfers", I read, "free divers, spear fishermen and blue water fishing experts. All have traveled the globe surfing, fishing and diving in pursuit of the Salt Lifestyle. Today, we live by our commitment to our original concepts and continue to visit places like the North Shore of Hawaii, Tavarua in Fiji, Indonesia, Central America, Venezuela, the Bahamas and other remote Salt Life locations on a regular basis."

Avid watermen sound perfect for a Wonder Voyage. I read on: "During our adventures, we assembled a team of hardcore watermen from every corner of the world. Through these very special individuals, we have established lifelong ties with the local experts in each region of the globe and made them part of the Salt Life family."

I need to find a Salt Life location. But it won't do to erect a deckchair outside and shout: "Come, I will make you the hardcore watermen of unAmericanism!" I'll need to pose as someone putting together an expedition.

One thing a lot of Americans share is a fierce pride in our Irish ancestry, so it'll be more credible to say I'm looking for watermen for a mission intent on proving that the Irish discovered America a thousand years before Columbus. Like the heroes of MTV's *Jackass* or Discovery's *Deadliest Catch*, we'll just have our masculinity and the clothes on our backs to help us prove that a leather-bellied coracle really can be paddled all the way across the ocean despite storms, deadly waves, huge whales, feral birds and looming icebergs.

My local Salt Life stockist is Willy's Sporting Goods in the Azaela Square Shopping Center. Googling the address, I notice that they just happen to be recruiting currently for the position of Athletic Apparel Associate.

"At Willy's Sporting Goods", says the ad, "our teammates work to play and play to work in an exciting environment that brings people together to provide our customers with the best shopping experience for the most authentic line of sporting goods and apparel."

They seem to have been trying to fill this position for some time, and I figure the "work to play, play to work" line is code for: "We don't pay much, but it's fun to work here, so what the hell?"

It won't be difficult to land this job. And Willy's Sporting Goods will be the ideal place to recruit twelve hardcore watermen.

3

Willy Douglas is a very old man dressed in tight denim. He reminds me of Buffalo Bill. I'm up in the windowless office above his Sporting Goods store, and for some reason I'm thinking of that Beatles line: "hold you in his armchair you can feel his disease."

I'm in an armchair, and I can feel Willy's disease, though I'm not quite sure what it is. Prostate cancer? Leukemia? Foot fungus? There's a medicinal scent lingering around the filing cabinet Willy is rifling through.

He pulls out a fat folder and turns menthol eyes on me. "Ever been a member of a union?" he demands gruffly, flicking a lock of lank, withered hair from his eyes.

"Nope."

Willy looks relieved, and throws himself back into a massive wheeled, spinning office chair. Just to be sure, though, he goes through the folder, checking off the unions one by one.

"The Amalgamated Clothing and Textile Workers Union? That mean anything to you?"

"No, sir."

"Union of Needletrades, Industrial and Textile Employees?"

"Never heard of them."

"That's UNITE to their friends, of which I am not one", says Willy, as if there could be any doubt. "How about the Retail, Wholesale and Department Store Union?"

"I am not a member of that either, Mr Douglas."

"Are you now, or have you ever been, a member of the Communist Party, Brad?"

"I have not, sir."

"I'm liking you more and more, boy. In fact, I'm prepared to give you the chance to work in my store. It's a place where hard work is its own reward."

"I'm very glad to hear that, sir. Thank you!"

"I should tell you how things work around here. We're a little unconventional. First thing to get straight is that we don't pay you."

"You, uh, don't pay me?"

"Not unless you shift over $2000 of sportswear a week, Brad, and I'll tell you quite frankly, you won't be doing that, not with things the way they are now. No, you're going to be paying us what we call an Opportunity Rental. It's a fee we take for letting you work our floor on a daily basis."

"I don't quite understand, sir."

"At Willy's Sporting Goods, we don't give you an old-fashioned wage. Instead, we give you a sporting chance to get rich", explains the proprietor, rotating his enormous chair with a squeak. "We could use slaves, like other companies do. But we prefer to employ white people. In exchange for your rental fee, we provide you with access to our regular stream of customers and encourage you to solicit them for payments of various kinds."

I say nothing. The walls and hanging strip lights seem closer now.

"We also have innovated away the deadly monotony of fixed working hours. At Willy's you'll be on an Anytime Contract. That means that we can call on you at any time and give you notice to come on down to the store within twenty minutes. Since we're a 24/7 operation, that could be any time of the day, or any time of the night. It all depends on demand. If we see customers coming, we call on the staff we require to deal with them. You will be a point-of-need responder, Brad. Like a firefighter or a lifeguard."

"I see. It sounds… interesting."

"Never a dull moment, boy! Now, as regards remuneration, you will be able to solicit that from the customers themselves in several ways. You can offer them coffee and muffins, for instance. Make it sound like it's on the house and then hit them with a bill when they've finished. Bringing the foodstuffs will be your own responsibility, or you can just get them from Starbucks and add any markup you consider reasonable. If you see customers heading for the toilet out in the mall, we will allow you to follow them with a tray of scented surfactants and unguents."

"I'm sorry?"

"Perfumes and soaps, boy, perfumes and soaps! You can sell them in the bathroom. You'll also be allowed to keep a small supply of gift candles to hand out to the ladies, which, again, you can charge them for as they leave the store. Should the police be summoned, we will back you. And finally, when you see the customers—possibly by this point disgruntled—headed for the car park, you will be permitted to follow them with a squeegee and a bucket of soapy water, and as they enter their vehicles you will be allowed to cleanse the windshield unbidden until they pay you to leave."

"What a… great series of opportunities, sir!"

"It's how I started myself, boy!"

I nod, surveying the shabby office furniture and outmoded Microsoft computers.

"When do I start?"

"Why, exactly twenty minutes after we call you!"

"Of course. You explained that."

Willy seems to approve of extracurricular motivations and ambitious schemes.

"Sir, I should tell you that one reason I want this job is to recruit extreme watermen—the kind attracted by your Salt Life line—for a sea voyage."

Willy looks delighted.

"That's good to know, Brad. I like your enterprise! That'll be a great topic with which to engage the customers in conversation. Of course, should your expedition make profits, you'll need to pay Willy's Sporting Goods a commission of 20%. Does that sound reasonable?"

"Perfectly reasonable, sir. I wouldn't have it any other way."

Damn you, Buffalo Bill!

4

In case you're reading this in some obscure part of the world still unfamiliar with the Confederate Attic Calendar, here's a list of months you may wish to consult as the narrative unfolds:

• Hekatombaion starts the year in what used to be called "July and August".

• Metageitnion, the second month, is what was known as "August and September".

• Boedromion, the third, was once called "September and October". Those are the three summer months.

• Pyanepsion begins autumn; in their slovenly way the ancestors called this month "bits of October and November".

• Maimakterion is what the ancients sloppily described as "November and December".

• Poseideon is the Attic Calendar's much more interesting name for what was once "December and January".

• Gamelion begins a cluster of three Arctic months: aeons ago this was "January and February".

• Anthesterion is what they used to call "February and March".

• Elaphebolion is the final winter month, corresponding to what surviving non-Confederates call "March and April".

• Mounichion sees the first sexual burst of spring: once termed "April and May".

• Thargelion is our proud name for the flushes, thrusts and pangs of what was once "May and June".

• Skirophorion ("June and July" anon) brings the year to fruition.

The CSA adopted this Greek calendar after the Victory of 1865, but could equally well have used the French revolutionary calendar, which slots three ten-day weeks into twelve months running from Vendémiaire (mid-September) to Fructidor (mid-August). It's funny how things turn out; at the time, something seems completely arbitrary, and yet with 20/20 hindsight it becomes difficult to imagine any other outcome.

5

It's the month of Metageitnion. The Canadian wild ginger flourishes by the side of the highway, its leaves gaily flapping now lanceolate, now tomentose. Four unusual visitors roll up to Tastee Freez in a Mercedes 600, a stately car with multiple hydraulic functions and air-compressed suspension.

"If you're merely someone", they say, "you have a Rolls-Royce. But if you're God you have a Mercedes 600." This old saw is typical of the sort of misconception people have about God, but when the elderly janitor sees the car crossing the Tastee Freez lot, the fallen divinity does experience a spasm of envy.

The four new arrivals have German accents, carry pen torches and drum the booth tabletop with their fingers. They "tsk" a bit when God starts sweeping around their feet, but soon forget him.

By the way, if you think that working at a Tastee Freez in South Carolina is too humble a position for God, you really haven't read your Bible. Christ washed his disciples' feet and tramped around unimportant villages in Galilee. Meanwhile, God lived in the comparative splendour of Mount Horeb, a place so obscure that no map records it today. God certainly can't remember where it is, what with his deteriorating mental condition.

"At least it was stored in an orderly way", says one of the men. His hair is carefully coiffed. "I wasn't so crazy about the stucco art nouveau ornaments", he continues, "but I appreciated the zigzag parquet. It creaked like the floor of an old castle, so I asked for a pair of felt slippers."

"Korrekt!" smiles the second, who has eyes as grey as the Baltic. It seems to be an in-joke, because the other three laugh.

"Speaking of the Mora Discotheque", says the third man, who looks like a cosmonaut, "this place reminds me of that milk bar on the Schneider Wibbel Gasse."

"That place where the waiters are international in origin?" asks the fourth man, who has the calm, epicene look of a pierrot.

"Exactly!"

"And there is hung the oil portrait of a narcissistic actor?"

"Korrekt!"

It's apparently not so amusing the second time around.

"What shall we order, Ralf?" asks the Baltic-eyed man.

"Isn't it the asparagus season, Florian? We ought to study the varieties of vegetable dishes on the menu in some detail", replies the one with stark modernist coiffure.

"Did you leave your Arriflex in the car, Wolfgang?" asks the cosmonaut.

"Yes, Karl. Do you think I should bring it in?"

"I think it's probably safe in the lot", says Karl. "The car's metalwork is bulletproof."

God is making himself as small and insignificant as possible, sweeping around their feet, keeping his white head down. Wolfgang is soldering white cable to two delicate sticks of oxidised brass using a battery-powered pocket soldering iron.

"What I hate about jet aircraft", he says to no one in particular, "is all the hot exhaust gases that get blown into the atmosphere".

"Next time we should perhaps take the train to America", observes Florian sardonically. "One of those nice oriental trains with intarsia work and mother-of-pearl inlays around the compartment ceiling."

"Isn't it time to clean our teeth?" asks Ralf, checking his elegant gold watch.

"My mother was most particular about lunchtime tooth-cleaning", agrees Wolfgang, adding: "But this should occur after the meal, not before."

"Of course", says Ralf. "Your mother, Hildegard, was always right about these things."

"I like the mannerisms of the waiter", says Florian, who is making perfunctory sketches in a small notebook. His hand movements are somewhat restricted by a pair of tight-fitting black gloves. His polo-necked sweater also appears to be a bit on the tight side, making his muscular physique in some ways perhaps too presentable.

"Do you think they will serve me a small dish of herring with parsley and cream?" asks Karl.

"Don't be ridiculous, Karl, this is America! Everything here is made with sugar", says Wolfgang.

"Well, do you think it will work if I say, 'A small dish of herring with parsley and cream, hold the sugar'?"

"Ah, what I would not do right now for some traditional Bavarian fare!" sighs Wolfgang.

A general despondency descends. Wolfgang finishes his soldering and pockets the iron.

"Why don't we just walk out of here and go cycling instead?" suggests Florian suddenly. "That way we can work up an appetite and then perhaps find a traditional steak lodge in the mountains later?"

This meets with general consent, and the four men leave a booth by now conspicuously cleaner than the others. God watches them unload push-bikes from the trunk of the car. He is already hatching plans to borrow the Mercedes 600.

6

I mentioned that my father was an archeologist in Bangkok. That was a lie.

In fact, Dad was a doctor. He was often called in to minister to the Catawba people up on the reservation.

The Catawba lived in bark houses with rounded tops. Since they had semi-autonomous status, the Catawba could license casinos and other gaming houses on their ancestral lands; this quickly became their main source of income. It was the white man's revenge on the Catawba, declared Dad, because otherwise their bad treatment would confer upon them an unbearable moral superiority.

"If they weren't doing something low-down and dirty like gambling", Dad said, "they'd be up there on the high moral ground, looking down on us."

A combination of shame, unemployment and chronic alcoholism made the Catawba a sorry tribe; many of their illnesses stemmed from depression, according to Dad. His solution was to prescribe the best modern medication, and lots of it.

"Dancing round a pole imitating a crow won't lift these good people out of the shit we've dropped them in", he'd say in his John Wayne-like drawl. "They deserve the best modern medicine has to offer".

A man from the reservation came to Dad complaining that he was inhabited by the spirit of a bear. Dad gave him a combination of Prothiaden and Aropax. Sure enough, after a couple of months not only had the imaginary bear departed, so had all the real bears that used to hang around the reservation, delving in the trash and causing a rumpus.

This, however, depressed the elders, who depended on bears for some of their rituals. Dad put them on Zoloft and Xanax, and soon the wrinkly old men were so cheerful that they not only stopped missing the bears, they stopped conducting religious ceremonies altogether.

Because of this, however, some of the aged women in the community, who were about to die, got very miserable, thinking that their souls were condemned to wander across dismal plains forever rather than head to paradise. Dad put the crones on Stelazine, Epilim and Effexor. It was such a success that not only did the women stop complaining about the lack of religious services, they stopped worrying about death and, in some cases, positively embraced it. Three of them used a shotgun, and four jumped off a low cliff.

By now I was really beginning to see the interconnectedness of all things. The younger women in the village mourned what they saw as the premature death of the old women. So Dad put them on Largactil, which is Chlorpromazine.

Interestingly enough, all the younger women experienced one of the drug's weirder side effects, evident in only 5% of the white women who take it: they experienced spontaneous whole-body orgasms when they sneezed. This was so good, in and of itself, that the women no longer saw any need for actual sex, and the tribe quickly died out.

This might have made Dad feel guilty, but he was taking high doses of Paxil and Prozac. All in all, he ended up feeling pretty good about things.

When a big leisure corporation turned the Catawba reservation into a golf course, Mom had some residual moral qualms, especially when we used to drive past there on the way to the farmer's market. So Dad gave her Resperidone, increased the dose after a week, and added a chaser of 300mg Tofranil tablets. Pretty soon Mom, too, was serene.

Then there was just me, preaching from the back seat, the family's moral voice. I was shut up with Ritilan and Elavil administered orally, plus Nortriptyline and Lithium fed by nocturnal intravenous drip.

Without the drugs we probably would have been so consumed with guilt that we'd never have dared mention the Catawba again. But on all that medication, basking in that glow of well-being, we felt balanced, perfectly able not just to refer to the disappeared indigenous tribes, but to take on some aspects of their lives.

Obviously nothing can ever replace the Catawba, their rituals, their worldview, their distinctive culture. That's gone now, forever. But we can revive—selectively, and according to our own whims—the nice bits of their society.

Mother is always the first up. She dresses the trims of the seal-oil lamp. Sizzling, the lamp burns brightly; it needs to, because our tree-bark house has no windows.

Father pulls on a bird-skin parka and enters the long passage that leads to the clearing where a low earthen roof conceals our dwelling of sod and wood.

Father scans the clouds and sky; the weather will determine whether he'll take the kayak out, string fish on a line to dry, or head up to the trading store to exchange ivory totems for stainless steel needles.

Up in the village meeting house sits Grandfather, chanting softly the thousand secret names of the wind. Under his tongue a white tablet of Wellbutrin XL dissolves slowly.

7

Metageitnion gives way to the cooler weather of Boedromion. In the hedgerows *Helianthemum carolinianum* becomes abundant, its pendules solitary, its calyx longer than its capsule. I've now mastered all the deceptions and aggravations Willy recommends, and added a few of my own:

1. CLOTHES MICROLEASING
When you head to the changing room to try on an item of apparel at Willy's, you probably miss the legal notice that informs you that what you're doing is "microleasing", and charges apply. That's because the notice is partly obscured by the two-way mirror I'm using to shoot softcore material to sell to gay websites. (I wouldn't have to do this if you guys tipped.)

2. SECONDARY SALES BEFORE PRIMARY
While trying to pay for the purple running pants you chose, you'll find yourself offered unrelated products at the till. Would you like personal injury insurance, a Samsonite-themed Chinese luggage set, or a three-speed smoothie juicer? There are up to twenty-six offers of unbeatable secondary-sale bargains to decide upon before you can pay for the pants. We believe in giving you all the choice in the world!

3. NON-STANDARD BAG
Under the counter there are two piles of carry bags, one free, the other not. They look (and in fact are) identical, but I add

the chargeable bag to all bills unless specifically instructed otherwise. It costs $2.99.

4. LOYALTY CARD
In order to apply for our loyalty card (printed and laminated at Kinko's), you must give me your full name, address, phone number, email and bank account number (for the promised direct bonus payments). I will then forward your details to an identity thief in Honduras who pays good money for this stuff.

5. FORTUNE-TELLING / NAIL SERVICE
Did you know that facts about your future can be derived from the state of your nails? Best keep them in good shape, then! I offer a combined fortune-telling and nail manicure service. At present this takes place at a fire assembly point. Your future improves at the exact same rate your nails do. Unless there's a fire.

Recruitment for the sea voyage, however, is not going so well. Willy's customers are universally overweight. Twelve of them would surely send my coracle straight to Davy Jones's locker.

There's great news, though: the store is to receive a visit from all four Salt Life founders! Even if their customers are slobs, the Salt Life guys themselves must have tight abs and fearsome waterman skills. They will arrive during the first full moon of Pyanepsion. I can't wait!

I've also made a new friend. Store Manager Randy Lee has become a bit of a mentor to me. If Willy's influence has been a malign one, Randy represents something benign and redemptive.

Randy's strength is people management; it feels like he can see right through you. If you bring him a conflict, he resolves it with sweetness and reason. Even if you've done something bad (I left the squeegee covered in squashed insects on Tuesday, for instance), Randy doesn't dress you down. Instead, he demonstrates compassion, non-violence, insight, effectiveness and uplift.

Randy is an Asian-American. I think his parents are Chinese, possibly Japanese. He is comfortably wide-bodied, with a round face and droopy eyebrows. He likes to sit in the back office with the aircon unit cascading its coolness over his shaved head.

Randy tells me he comes from a privileged family, but has renounced all his entitlements, choosing instead to do a simple job at Willy's. He says it gives him a clarity he couldn't otherwise achieve. He refuses all forms of payment, and sleeps on a bed of moss under a tree in Azalea Park.

The luxury with which Randy was surrounded while growing up has convinced him that material wealth, indulgence and involvement represent nothing but pain. Randy was addicted to every harmful substance known to man, he ran with gangs for a while, dealt drugs, pumped himself full of shit, quaffed Jim Beam, killed a man and travelled the darkest corridors of his mind like a roller coaster.

But Randy has emerged clean. He's a fully-rounded human being thanks to intensive meditation. Sometimes I swear he's omniscient.

One day we're rearranging a display of ladies' DryMesh shorts when Randy flips a rainbow-piped grey pair out of the rail and says: "The 65% cotton content in these shorts was harvested in Tajikistan by a schoolgirl called Oisha then shipped to Bangladesh. There it was machined by an overworked mother of three called Nishat. You might remember how a garment trade building collapsed last year in Dhaka? It made all the papers. Well, Nishat's workshop is just around the corner."

I ask Randy how he knows these details. He answers that they aren't strictly true, but might as well be.

"Had this pair of shorts been packed in the next box", he continues, "it would have been shipped to Osaka, Japan, where it would have been sold at a new discount outlet called Shimomura to a twelve-year-old girl called Masako. One day Masako, wearing the piped shorts, leaps astride her pink bicycle and cycles to a dolphinarium flanked by two large video screens showing advertisements and public announcements, including police Most Wanted ads. Amongst the criminal mug shots flashed up on the video screens Masako suddenly recognises the face of her own father, who disappeared two years ago. She is shocked to see him listed as a dangerous sex offender."

"Say!" I holler, admiringly. "That's very interesting, Randy! And quite plausible!"

Randy's kind of tale—not true, but might as well be—certainly helps pass time on the sales court. I find myself adopting the habit, which I'm tempted to call Speculative Realism.

8

It's Pyanepsion. Yellow corymb creeps through ditches, stellular in pubescence, flower-crowded.

I am buying two frozen pizzas. A boy behind me in the supermarket check-out line suddenly bursts out: "Excuse me, sir, but are you wearing a fake wig?"

I explain patiently that there's no such thing as a fake wig, since all wigs are real wigs.

The boy shakes his head.

"An actor in a movie whose role demands a wig could fake it by using his own hair."

"So are you suggesting that I'm using my real hair to fake a wig?"

This is clearly not what the boy intended to suggest, but stubbornness makes him pretend that it is.

"Yes, sir. I believe you're using your real hair as a fake wig."

To prove that the wig I'm wearing is real, I lift it off my head: "There. You see, kid, it's a real wig."

The boy turns to a female behind him and says: "I told you he was wearing a wig!"

I've been tricked and am now the object of general conversation. An old man turns to the boy and says: "He could still be using his real hair as a fake wig. All he'd have to do is detach his real hair from his head first, then lift it clean off his head like a wig."

Normally this kind of disrespect would make me furious. But today I am swelling with pride. I have been selected to extend an official Willy's welcome to the four ardent watermen and facilitate the passage of Salt Life's founding fathers through Columbia Metropolitan Airport. Even just writing these words, I am trembling.

The logistical challenges alone are hair-raising. It is my duty to smoothly expedite the directors' journey from Columbia to Summerville for their historic visit to Willy's Sporting Goods. This represents a total distance of 96.5 miles. Anything might happen.

Let me say at the outset how much I have come to admire the Four Directors in the months since I met God at Tastee Freez. Making daily trips to the library, I have devoured all the available literature about their lives: their genesis, their years of self-help, their struggles with nemeses, competitors and detractors, their studies at the feet of gurus, their travels through the watery antipodes, battling monsters and bagging prizes, their alliance with Lady Fortuna, their defeat of the final Herculean foe, the solemn scene in which they signed their names in Fate's ledger, deep in the glimmering caves of Valhalla, their long search for experts, strong watermen and other followers, their alliances with the Powerful Ones, the clashing thunderbolts of Zeus and Thor, the final apotheosis of the Four Directors via the just establishment of their leisurewear empire, and finally the present chapter, encompassing commercial zenith, expansion, unresisted universalisation, sanctification, teachings, hagiographies, veneration, deification.

Perhaps because of the comparative wealth of material available on their early struggles, I have come to admire the Four Directors more than God, of whose origin very little is known. I think of theirs as a more American story: a fourfold success born of vision, unity, will and effort. For all his affected humbleness, God is a more lofty, lonely, aristocratic figure. More European. I doubt God ever really had to overcome much. He certainly never had a business success, unless we count the Roman Catholic church. I think of him as a champagne socialist, born with a silver spoon in his mouth, waving his wand according to urges that come and go, making and smashing worlds on a toddler's whim.

Don't get me wrong, I'm not turning my back on God. But imagine the New World of the Salt Life directors in the service of God's ancien régime! That's my dream. Their husky followers have disappointed me. The thing to do now is think bigger, go to the source.

I plan to recruit the Four Directors themselves to the Wonder Voyage, complemented by eight mighty watermen of their choosing. I owe God the very best.

But my plans are temporarily thrown off course by a piece of horrible, horrible news. Randy Lee has been murdered.

According to the feds who called at the store today, it happened while he was sitting serenely under his tree in Azalea Park. Five crackheads wielding razors and chains suddenly approached and demanded money. The dialogue that ensued has been reported by a confederate who ratted on his friends as part of a plea deal. The feds, surrounding a shoe display, act out the scene for us right here in the store.

"Guys", says Randy, "I have no money. I have set myself free from money, and you can do the same." (The person playing Randy at this point is actually a policewoman.)

The gang circle the moss seat at the base of the tree. (The feds tighten their circle around the display showcasing the new Nike HTM Flyknit collection.)

"Check him for weapons", commands the ringleader. (In the store, the lead investigator.)

"Leave him alone!" cries the gang member who later ratted. (Remember, we only have the rat's word for this.)

"Shut up", snarls the ringleader at the rat (played by a junior police officer who looks a lot like Lee Harvey Oswald), "or we'll kill you too!"

"You're going to kill me?" asks Randy Lee (now played by a fat male Irish cop). "You know that killing is wrong, right?"

"Yes!" shouts the rat, "he's right: killing is wrong!"

At this, three of the gang members (played by feds) grab the rat and pin him to the ground. The ringleader goes up to the slave patrolman now playing Randy and shoots him in the belly.

"That's murder!" shouts the rat, but he's silenced by a rainfall of blows, which mysteriously all miss, leaving his face and body without lasting marks.

Randy, now played by Buffalo Bill, dies.

After the feds have gone, we stand holding hands in a circle around the Nike Flyknit display and observe a two-minute silence in memory of Randy. I remain in front of the presentation video alone for a further eighteen minutes, weeping silently and meditating on transience.

Later, I will argue to Willy that a permanent monument should be made in the store to commemorate our fallen comrade. I will suggest that a video of Randy's aphorisms (discovered in a Word file on his work computer) should play on a continuous loop in the middle of the Nike display. Willy will agree to this, but insist that the standard Nike Flyknit video replace the aphorisms.

"Then when we watch that video", he says, "we'll just each privately think about Randy rather than Nike."

I will accept this compromise. Life is short.

9

The Watermen's aircraft seems to float weightless in the night sky for several minutes as it arrives from the west. The small, pointed faces of the musicians of the Spartanburg High School Marching Band are raised one by one to the clear night sky.

"Unknown constellations sparkle into view", I tell myself, "white as milk, dry as teeth in skulls."

"Here is the bank of the Curlew River", I tell myself.

"Known constellations are temporarily altered by the passage of clouds and mists", I tell myself, as if it were something the sage Li Bai used to say.

"The perilous sound of the lyre rings throughout the land", I mutter, forebodingly.

"Yet a propitious breeze is lifting", I reassure myself, "and a great book is being written, chapter and verse".

"Aslan is on the move!" I add. And: "Ferryman, do you have a place for me?"

I'm listening to Benjamin Britten's opera *Curlew River* on my iPod, attempting to drown out the sound of the Spartanburg High School Marching Band. I tried to get the University of South Carolina Marching Band, but they were booked to perform *Thus Spake Zarathustra* in a shopping mall.

The Spartanburgers' hearts are in the right place, but unfortunately they haven't quite mastered their instruments yet. What's more, it's way past their bedtime. It must be 3am!

A god-almighty hullabaloo ensues when the band begins the piece I've asked them to prepare: Handel's *Music for the Royal Fireworks*. It sounds like a tailback in Cairo. But it'll have to do.

In a blast of thunder and a spiral of dust the charter 747 arrives, slows, and taxis to a halt. Waiting steps are rushed into position, the front door of the massive craft opens slowly, and the Four Directors range themselves on the top step for the official photograph.

What a surprise! They are old! And tiny! And frail!

Like a geriatric rock band, the Watermen are wearing identical suits in slate grey, teal blue, clay brown and devil black, each with a white handkerchief peeping over the breast pocket. They have spectacles on. Their hair, brushed severely back across their skulls and gelled down, nevertheless flutters in the wind. They raise paper-thin hands in a feeble salute. Their lips are curly, their eyes milky. They remind me of elderly Jewish obstetricians.

I wave a hand, and the band strikes up. It sounds like a herd of braying donkeys stampeding through a canyon.

Unsteady of foot and unsure of balance, the four old men sway down the metal steps. Can these really be my Watermen? My heroes? Apparently so. Somewhere God is chuckling.

After bending to shake their tiny hands and blurting some official words of welcome, I bundle the Watermen into one of the waiting cars. The other won't be needed, and I signal it away; the Watermen are so small that all four fit on a single back bench. I take the front seat and direct the driver.

Too bitter and disappointed to converse with the guests, I take a Rubik's Cube from my briefcase and hand it back wordlessly. The Watermen appear never to have seen one, and pass it from hand to hand in delight, nudging elbows, pointing excitedly, scratching heads.

We head east on Airport Boulevard towards Aviation Way, turn left into Lexington Drive, take the first right onto John N. Hardee Expressway, then left onto Airport Boulevard. From the Charleston-bound I-26 we exit to US-17, which leads us all the way to Summerville. There's very little traffic at this time of night, and we arrive in front of Willy's at 4.25am.

As I open the door for them, the smiling Watermen hand me back my Rubik's Cube, a solid colour on each of its six sides.

10

When he sees what inconsequential little squirts they are, even Willy ignores the Watermen. They're parked on a stool in the shoe-fitting area, and sit there obediently, saying and doing nothing. A few early-bird customers mill around, probably mistaking the Watermen for garden ornaments. When the car comes to pick them up, I'm like: "Yeah, whatever, dudes, enjoy the rest of your short lives".

When they've gone, I spend an hour or two engulfed in regret. Why did I invest so much in all that trash, those business biographies about the rise, strategy, and philosophy of those pathetic gnomes? It becomes clear that I was simply project-ing—in grotesquely inappropriate directions—my own inner need for heroes.

What would Randy say? "Be the Waterman you wish to see in the world." But I'm through with Watermen. It's too late.

The following day Willy promotes me to Randy's old job. No more squeegee, no more perfumes and soaps for me!

I soon discover that Randy had hardly any duties in the store. All he was required to do was potter around in his back office most of the day, tour the sales court once in a while, witness the daily deposit with Mrs Mendoza in the cash office, and negotiate with visiting company reps. The rest of his time Randy devoted to composing aphorisms (the Word file on his computer runs to 40,000 words) and making up alternative histories of things. Speculative Realism.

It's actually a really nice position. Sure, there's still no pay, but life attains a rich, slow dignity in the back office.

One day I'm sent to check out the stock at Prima Dance Apparel and Formalwear on South Main Street. Willy wants to know if they have any fast-moving lines we could adopt. It's an undercover mission, because if Prima suspected Willy's was going to duplicate their best lines they'd be furious.

In order to arouse as little suspicion as possible, I disguise myself as a Prussian nobleman of the early 19th century. My daughter, I explain to the lady behind the counter, wishes to be a ballerina.

"Vhat are zee most popular items for zpoiled children of this zort?" (I say "zpoiled" with a teasing twinkle in my eye, and a finger on the tip of my joke store moustache.)

The Prima proprietor isn't fooled for a moment. "You cleaned my windshield at Willy's!" she exclaims. "I know who you are! Get out of my store!"

I slink out, pausing at the door only to click my heels and make a military salute followed by a deep bow. "I vill tell my daughter to adopt another pastime", I say, hoping to make the lady feel guilty. "She vill veep."

Removing the moustache outside, I notice some junk in the window of the unmarked store next door. Something about it looks interesting. Reflexively, I put the moustache back on.

Nobody seems to be inside the junk store. I soon notice that everything on sale reflects the taste of one person, someone extremely unlike the typical Summerville resident. The contents are principally books, but also men's clothes, vinyl records, coins from many countries, wallets, spectacle frames, old cameras and other personal effects. Snapping into Speculative Realist mode, I start to piece together a cover story.

Bernard Hermann was a humanist scholar who left South Carolina in his twenties to study in Paris. He'd dreamed of befriending Jean-Paul Sartre, but ended up giving English lessons in Montrouge, an undistinguished southerly suburb of the city. He began to visit Shakespeare and Co., the legendary Left Bank bookstore run by George Whitman, hoping to run into one of the writers from the Beat Hotel. In the cramped, murky aisles he discovered a treasury of modern German literature in translation. Hermann devoured works by Martin Walser, Robert Musil, Max Frisch, Günter Grass, Bertolt Brecht, Thomas Mann and Heinrich Boll. After forty years in Paris, he developed a terminal illness and returned to Summerville. By the time the ship carrying his books and other personal effects reached America, Hermann (whose elderly brother owned a vacant store on South Main Street) was dead.

Just as I'm completing this biographical sketch, Hermann's brother shuffles through from the back. "All books a dollar", he says.

The intrusion startles me. Assuming the Prussian accent again, I pick up the first book that comes to hand and say: "I veel take zees, zank yoo ferry much, zir."

"Do you want it wrapped?" asks the senior citizen, regarding me curiously over half-moon glasses.

"No sank yoo."

I throw the paperback down on the passenger seat of my Dodge. "Peter Handke", the cover reads, *An Essay on Tiredness*.

Over the next few days, bored at work, I start reading the Handke essay in my back office and find captivating its idea that tiredness is a way of escaping both socialisation and separation. I try to sleep less at night in order to experience at Willy's the delicious derangement of my senses which tiredness brings about, just as Handke's narrator does in church as a boy.

Soon I am luxuriating in my exhaustion, feeling myself transformed into a kind of passive goldfish as Willy's customers mull the purchase of shoes they'll never wear for sports, or congregate by the video screens watching games they'll never play on MSG Plus.

11

Odorata, orbiculate-leafed, drifts malignantly on the surface of stagnant pools, tuberous, nodose and woody.

The are some odd houses in Summerville. I mean, they present themselves oddly to the street.

Cycling around the hood I notice a plaster statuette on a passing lawn depicting the famous Belgian Piss Mannequin. You know the one: a bulbous-bellied little boy stands naked, urinating proudly. This version, like the original in Brussels, has a constant stream of water cascading from a tiny plaster penis. But here the naughty little fountain imp is lit by a harsh white strobe light.

Just... Why?

As I'm passing the house the door opens and a dog runs out, barking. It's soon snapping around my ankles. It's only a small dog, nothing really threatening, but it's enough to make me stop. The dog is followed by its owner, a thin bearded man who looks like a cross between DH Lawrence and Captain Haddock from the *Tintin* stories.

"Saville! Saville!" shouts the man, "Come away! Leave him alone!"

The stoop-chested fellow grabs the wiry little mongrel's collar and apologises to me with a shy smile. Something about him suggests confidence and collusion. I get an urge to strike up a conversation.

"I was just admiring your Piss Mannequin!"

"Oh, that! I inherited that from the previous owner, who picked it up on a visit to Belgium. I just added the strobe light."

"It's certainly eye-catching! Have you lived here long?"

"Just a couple of months. I was in Berlin before, but the rents are going up there, and I heard rumours that you could get houses here really cheap. It turns out to be true!"

"Yeah, times are hard. A lot of folk bought houses they couldn't afford, got them repossessed by the banks, who dumped them for peanuts."

"That's exactly what happened here", confides the shining-eyed young man. "But instead of kicking the previous owner out, I allowed him to share the place with me. I don't need so much room myself. As for the aesthetics, we compromise: he gets to keep his Piss Mannequin if I get to choose how it's lit, that kind of thing."

"What an incredible arrangement! And incredibly enlightened, from an ethical point of view!" I enthuse. The young man seems pleased and holds out his hand.

"Jan", he says, "Jan Lindenberg. And this is Saville, my dog. Named after Peter Saville, the graphic designer."

Saville, bemused by the attention, dances in a circle at our feet.

"Why don't you come in for a glass of Turkish tea?"

"I'd love to!"

I lock my bike and follow Jan inside.

"I'd like you to meet Frank, my housemate", says Jan, indicating a statuesque figure sunk in a big chair. Frank glances up from the fish tank, then resumes his viewing.

"Frank used to watch a lot of TV", says Jan, "but we agreed it wasn't good for him. So I've encouraged him to watch the fish instead. I believe he's a good deal happier as a result."

"Cosign, Jan, all the way", I smile. "Those moronic reality shows, punctuated by endless commercials, the celebs, the running news making you feel like humanity is totally shitty... Really, who needs TV?"

"Frank", says Jan in a loud voice, "would you like a Turkish tea? I'm just putting the kettle on for Brad here."

"Pepsi!" Frank says.

"What's that? PEPSI? Now Frank, you know we don't drink Pepsi in this house", chides Jan. "But I'll tell you what. You can put a LITTLE SUGAR in your Turkish tea today, all right?"

Frank doesn't respond. He doesn't seem terribly happy here, but I guess there's not much he can do.

"Diabetes mellitus type 2", whispers Jan as he disappears into the kitchen.

While Jan makes the tea I scan the living room. It's kind of fun to work out which artefacts are Frank's and which Jan's. It's not that hard, actually. There's a Bob Ross painting—well, school of, anyway—depicting a gorgeous mountain reflected in a lake. Around it are arranged six monoprints by Lucy Skaer in an installation called *Fabrication* that also includes a table. I happen to know that Lucy originally intended this work to be called *The Table and Lies About It*. The prints are all taken from shapes in

48

the surface of the table.

Bob Ross is total kitsch, but he was certainly a dab hand at foliage.

"That's a lovely landscape", I say to Frank, trying to speak loudly and clearly, since he appears to be hard of hearing.

"Yup", snaps Frank.

Jan returns with three glasses of tea on a silver tray.

"I was just saying to Frank, that's a lovely landscape", I tell Jan.

"It really comes alive in the context of the Lucy Skaer installation", agrees Jan. "You know, when I first moved to Berlin in the nineties there used to be a Bob Ross painting store right on the corner of Alte Schoenhauserstrasse and Munzstrasse. He was huge in Germany. Of course now that whole area has been gentrified. The Bob Ross shop is long gone. You can't stop progress, I guess."

"And Bob Ross is dead!" I laugh. "The yuppies killed him!"

"That isn't even a joke", says Frank, his peevish voice quivering. "Bob Ross died of a broken heart. He was such a kind man, and the way the art world was going, favouring conceptual trash over painting skills and the appreciation of natural beauty… Well, there wasn't much for Bob to live for any more."

"Here's your tea, old man", says Jan, affectionately. "And this is for you too."

He hands the slave a sugar bowl.

12

It is now late Maimakterion. The eastern purple cone flower—
inwardly hairy and bulging at the middle—contracts at the
throat, its tube ventricose, its appendix erect.

I've been chatting with Preciosa Mendoza, the accountant. She
tells me her relations with Willy have been strained ever since
she mentioned to him one day, out of the blue, that her sister
Dolorosa got her arm horribly mangled while working a loom
at the home they share.

Now, Willy has a religious side. He likes to pose as a philanthro-
pist and do "good works" from time to time, as long as they
don't cost him any money. So he offered to employ the disabled
Dolorosa Mendoza at the store on a starting rate of zero
dollars. "If she proves useful", he said, "I might even have
some money for her at the end of the year."

Preciosa Mendoza duly reported this to her sister, who showed
up at the store the very next day, an empty sleeve pinned to
her side where her left arm used to be. She was set to work as
a store detective.

Willy liked Dolorosa's work, although not enough to pay her
for it "just yet". But one day a serious altercation happened in
the store: Dolorosa caught a young man in a hoodie trying to
steal six pairs of Frog brand flippers. When the kid fled, she
gave chase. The pair ended up in the car park, where the boy

pulled Dolorosa's left leg clean off before flippering across a pond and disappearing in the general direction of the Banfield Pet Hospital.

Because this tragedy began on his premises, Willy could hardly refuse Dolorosa's request to come back to work as soon as she'd completed her medical treatment and physiotherapy (which he was legally obliged to pay for). But he was clearly uncomfortable watching his store detective hauling herself around his sales court with just one arm and one leg, clinging to the legs of display units to drag herself across the shiny lino (which wasn't always entirely clean, unfortunately).

"What is this", Willy mumbled, his teeth clamped and gritty, "a freak show? She looks like a flesh rhombus!"

Worse was to come. Dolorosa arrived at work one day with no right arm either. She explained that there'd been a serious traffic accident on Bear Island Road, near the fire station. A flying car had narrowly missed her, removing her arm as it passed. The driver, unconscious in the aftermath, remembered nothing.

To help the now one-limbed Dolorosa get around the store and keep an eye on customers, the handyman—old Jack Brandt— made a sort of extra-large skateboard, attaching a set of low-friction wheels to a sheet of ply. Dolorosa could propel herself with her one extant leg if she was strapped tightly to the ply with a belt, her face pointing forward.

The system actually had some advantages: she was now so low, and the wheels were so smooth, that shoplifters could neither see nor hear her coming. Her productivity rate increased, and Willy was forced to promise a pay review in October.

In September, however, the unthinkable happened: Dolorosa lost her fourth and sole-remaining limb. The exact circumstances are unclear; at first she reported that a buzzard, turkey, vulture or carrion crow had attacked her and flown off with the leg, but later she admitted that she'd been trying to cut a young Douglas fir for a Christmas tree when slippery saliva had caused the saw in her mouth to engage her leg just where it connected to the trunk.

When she recovered, Dolorosa was adamant that she would continue her store detective job. She was fat enough that she could roll around the store like a ball, navigating the aisles much faster than she ever could on the skateboard. She wasn't able to arrest criminals—this now had to be done by old handyman Jack—but she was catching them faster than ever.

Then one evening something bizarre occurred. Willy was out drinking at BJ's Tavern when he saw Dolorosa sitting in a booth with a man. She had two arms and two legs, just like everyone else. Willy considered firing her right there on the spot—she was only employed because she was disabled, after all—but decided instead to play a longer game. Pretending he'd noticed nothing, he left the bar.

The next day at the store Willy got on the intercom and called Dolorosa to his office. She rolled up, wheezing, and declined the proffered chair with a reproachful glance.

"I get the feeling your health is improving", said Willy.

"Do you, sir? That's strange, because I reckon it's getting worse", Dolorosa replied.

Willy came suddenly to the point. "Didn't I see you at BJ's Tavern last night with a man and all your limbs?"

"You most certainly did not", spat Dolorosa, her eyes aflash. "Last night I was at holy mass at Saint John the Beloved. And I haven't had limbs for almost a year now. What are you... even saying?"

There was nothing for it but to back down. "I'm sorry", said Willy, "my mistake."

In fact Dolorosa *had* been at BJ's, drinking with a man she'd met on OKCupid. She'd still had all her limbs at that point. But now they've all been amputated; keeping her four extremities so tightly tucked and tied up inside her clothes while she was at work ruined Dolorosa's circulation, causing gangrene to spread through her arms and legs with lethal speed.

Preciosa tells me that Willy believes she was in on Dolorosa's deception, right up until the moment it became, tragically and ironically, a deception no longer. But Preciosa swears this isn't so; one reason the gangrene spread so fast was that Dolorosa maintained the illusion of disability at home, hiding her able body from her sister until it was able no more.

Now you can find Dolorosa most evenings begging outside Saint John the Beloved, Summerville's Catholic church. PLEASE HELP, reads the cardboard sign propped in front of her ball-like body, LOST ALL FOUR LIMBS. TWICE.

13

Just as it helps to know that the American Revolution began with a set of grievances against the British crown, so you may find it interesting to ground my grievances in my body type, and the personality type that goes with it. Know, then, that I am an extreme ectomorph, and that my nature is cerebrotonic.

I'm nothing more than an alert and anxious skeleton covered in skin. "All air and nerve", as Robert Lowell once put it. Now, American culture looks down on thin people just as it does on poor people. Hence my sense of grievance.

I became aware of the profound ramifications of my body type thanks to the American theorist William Sheldon. In the 1940s, Sheldon set forth what seems at first like a very simple way to measure body types. He isolates three basic components: fatness, muscularity and thinness, which he calls endomorphy, mesomorphy and ectomorphy. Every human body contains some measure of these qualities, which are all required to make it function.

"Ectomorphy means linearity, fragility, flatness of the chest and delicacy throughout the body", Sheldon wrote. "We find a relatively scant development of both the visceral and the somatic structures. The ectomorph has long, slender, poorly muscled extremities with delicate pipe-stem bones. He also has, relative to his mass, the greatest surface area and therefore the greatest sensory exposure to the outside world. He is thus in one sense overly exposed and naked to the world."

Nervous! Super-alert! Naked to the world!

After publishing his *Atlas of Men*, Sheldon moved on to his most interesting book, *The Varieties of Temperament*. In it he makes a link between body type and character. Using the same typology, he develops personality correlates for the body types. Panther-like mesomorphs are somatotonics, creatures of action. "In contrast to the emotional extraversion of the viscerotonic, the somatotonic shows extraversion in his actions. He hates to sit still, likes movement and exercise. Nothing gives him more pleasure than removing barriers that stand in his way and exploring the limits of his strength. He is competitive, has a loud voice and can behave recklessly. Little inclined to reflection, he may appear callous and tactless."

The ectomorph is by temperament a cerebrotonic. In ectomorph-cerebrotonics, "the sensory-receptor properties are well developed. As a consequence however the central nervous system is soon overloaded and rapidly tires. The cerebrotonic has the gift of concentrating his attention on the external world as well as on his internal world. His vigilance and autonomic reactivity make him behave in an inhibited and uncertain way: introverted behaviour. He has problems with expressing his feelings and with establishing social relationships, and can very well bear to be alone. The elementary strategies of coping with life are perception, reconnaissance and vigilance, cognition and anticipation, and a certain amount of privacy."

"The essential characteristic of the cerebrotonic is his acuteness of attention. The other two major functions, the direct visceral and the direct somatic functions, are subjugated, held in check, and rendered secondary. The cerebrotonic eats and exercises to attend."

And the leopards kick sand in his eyes!

14

"Brad Power to CEO! Brad Power to CEO!"

It's Willy Douglas calling me up to his office.

"Brad! Sit down. I was just wondering how that sea voyage of yours is shaping up?"

Willy has his eye on that 20%, no doubt.

"Not so good, sir. I'm not seeing the calibre of man I would need on such a voyage."

"The age of Iron John is gone", sighs Willy. "I'm talking about the early 1990s, of course. But there have been other ages of rugged exploration, during which men, lured by gold, rode the heaving ocean. Do you know what a cosmographer is, Brad?"

"I do not, sir!"

"A cosmographer is a describer of worlds. The breed—a fevered type of writer—flourished in the 16th century, that age of high adventure on higher seas. Some cosmographers were landlubbers, armchair men. Others rode the waves, writing with one hand, slaying painted natives with the other."

"Admirable, sir!" I don't really find such behaviour admirable, but Willy is the boss. He butters my bread. Or would, if he paid me.

"Well, they weren't always admirable, Brad. Just like the liberal media of today, they told lies. They were embedded reporters, hacks, *flâneurs*. They made up stories to please their listeners, whether that was the sucker sponsoring the next voyage or the gullible public eager to hear about precious metals, monsters and monopods. They weren't even all that brave, because staying home in a Europe ravaged by wars, plagues and famines was just as risky as heading off towards *terra incognita*."

Willy reaches across the messy papers on his desk and, grabbing a fat book, tosses it over to me. *The Singularities of Antarctic France, otherwise known as America, and of several lands and islands discovered in our time by Brother André Thevet, native of Angouleme, published in Paris in 1558*, it says on the front.

"That's a long title, sir. I don't think I ever heard of Antarctic France."

"It's down there", says Willy, pointing at the store's south wall. "Come on, let's ambulate."

As we walk, Buffalo Bill pontificates about Antarctic France.

"In Rouen, in October 1550, a simulacrum of Brazil was mounted for Henry 11 and Catherine de Medici on the banks of the Seine. In the green shade of a virgin forest rustling with parrots, monkeys and rare birds, three hundred actors—including fifty indians recently imported from Brazil—presented a vision of "the life of the savages". Toupinamba and Tamoyo indians worked, sang, danced, cooked, slept in hammocks, simulated lovemaking and warfare, all totally naked. Catherine de Medici came back several times on horseback to get her fill."

"It must have been fascinating, sir."

"You have to understand that by this point French mariners

had been plying back and forth between Rouen and Brazil for over fifty years", Willy tells me, charting a route around the imaginary monument to Randy Lee. "Some say Captain Jean Cousin discovered the New World in 1488, four years before Columbus."

"Sir, there are others who believe the Irish discovered the New World in the 6th century. They called it Tír na nÓg, the earthly paradise beyond the western horizon. Saint Brendan arrived there after a Wonder Voyage through an archipelago of extraordinary islands."

Willy seems mildly interested. "What kind of islands?"

"Well, sir, according to *The Voyage of Saint Brendan*, an island of sheep, an island of whales, an island of psalm-singing birds, an island of eternally young, bread-eating monks, an island with a well of forgetfulness, a coagulated sea, and some battling sea monsters—"

(We are temporarily separated by a row of changing rooms which cause Willy to miss some of the list.)

"—an island of fruit-eating anchorites, an island of grapes, a stretch of water where gryphons skirmished with birds, a volcano, an island where Judas was allowed a short holiday from Hell, an island where Paul the Hermit sat, dressed only in ground-length hair and fed by an otter—"

"Bull*SHIT*!" snarls Willy, catching up. "Fed by an otter?"

We suddenly notice four rancid old men clustered around the leotard section, deep in conversation.

"Shoplifters?"

"Old men like that, stealing leotards? I doubt it", says Willy. We edge closer, trying to overhear.

Willy gives a start of recognition: "It's ZZ Top!" he whispers. "And the guy with them is Hulk Hogan!"

ZZ Top have their trademark beards, which are knotted at their belts to avoid trailing the ground. Hogan, his face decorated with a horseshoe mustache, seems to be busting out of too-small clothes: sawn-off denim hot pants and a pink tank top. His tattoos depict machine guns and a bust of Hegel. The men all wear wraparound mirror shades.

"These would be the ideal guys to take on your voyage", whispers Willy. I nod, unconvinced. How could this most American of bands lead a mission to un-Americanise the world?

The men are discussing Michel Foucault's early enthusiasm for the Iranian revolution. Lead vocalist Billy Gibbons says that as far as he's concerned Foucault can "eat a bag of dicks" for giving the clerics a free pass. Bassist Dusty Hill agrees, arguing that Foucault clearly had a blind spot about feminism and underestimated the Ayatollah Khomeini's homophobia.

"We shoulda nuked Iran in 1979, gotten it over with", offers drummer Frank Beard.

Hulk Hogan begs to differ, and launches into a passionate defence of Foucault. "You guys were busy promoting your *Deguello* album in 1979, so maybe you lost track of geopolitics. Thing is, the Iranians had been under the American jackboot for years. Just like the Congolese and countless others since, the Iranian people had voted for a leftist named Mossadegh in their first ever democratic elections, only to have the CIA sponsor a coup against him. The guy was planning to nationalise the oil companies, see? So power went back to the Shah, the West's puppet. The Ayatollah represented an alternative with real spiritual authority. 'Scuse my French, but you can fuck identity politics up the butt with a limp jalapeño. What Foucault saw so clearly was that the radical Islamists, who were supported at that point by the Tehran University students and most of the progressive left, were Iran's best hope to throw off the American yoke, not to mention the inequality, corruption and sheer terror of the Shah's police state."

"Shoulda nuked Kent State, too", mutters drummer Beard.

Now Willy makes his move. "Gentlemen", he says, beaming, "I am the owner of this store. Is there something I can help you with today?"

"We were looking for leotards", says vocalist Billy, gruffly. "Can't get 'em our size in Texas."

"May I say what a delight and a privilege it is to have you here with us, gentlemen", Willy gushes. "I have all your albums!" He turns to Hogan, adding: "And all your fights!"

Billy doesn't seem friendly. "OK, dude, back off and give us some space."

"We're Texan musicians", explains Dusty, "we burn up the interstate in our hot rods, we play our guitars and shoot our guns, we owe our allegiance to the blue-collar everyman and, to tell the truth, we don't much care for entreprenoors like you." (That's the way he says it: entrepren*oooooooooooors*.)

"That's right. We are socialists", emphasises Hogan, looming threateningly. "If you're not part of the solution you're part of the problem. And you're no part of the solution, man."

Only Frank Beard looks conciliatory. As we back away, bowing, he scratches his dick through his leotard and winks.

15

It's during the chilly month of Poseideon—the Hairy Aster, its panicle few-flowered, has long since withered—that I first discover that the Willy's handyman, Jack Brandt, has his entire family living with him in the glass-walled utilities cubicle. And that they're illegal immigrants from Nicaragua.

I wrestle with a moral dilemma: whether or not to reveal their existence to the authorities.

I'm working the late shift one night. It's about 3am and nobody's in the store. I'm reading a book of Indian love poetry by candlelight. This is necessary because Willy has installed motion detecting lights to save electricity; only when a customer is approaching do the store's expensive electrical systems spring into life. From time to time I hear a scuffling sound as Dolorosa, the limbless store detective, rolls around in the dark, bulbous as a beach ball. (Did I mention that Willy, finding her begging one freezing day outside the church, took pity on Dolorosa and reinstated her?)

When the first scream breaks into my consciousness, the poet I'm perusing is Bhartrihari, the ancient master of the courtly love lyric. With my left leg I gently pump the shruti box I purchased to complement the elegant verse. A wheezing drone fills the back office as I read the Sanskrit words aloud softly, my own voice moving me deeply. This is a rough translation:

Their desire asleep, noble women, far from wanton
Are wont to block my unfurling tendril!
Yet, as desire impatiently probes they blush, loosen, yawn
And when, giving in to urgency, each one submits
To my "must" and "will" and "now", these noble women
In that critical moment, all enjoy
My stroking, caressing, breast-fondling, deep kissing
And all my other foreplay, very much indeed!

But before I tell you about the scream, and properly parse the poetry it interrupted, and speak of how I discovered this poetry in so unlikely a setting, I would like to mention an odd anecdote from the life of Bhartrihari. He was a king as well as a poet, and so devoted to his wife, Pingala, that not even nutcrackers could pry him from her bedroom.

One day the poet-king was gifted a magical fig that could extend his life sevenfold. He gave Pingala the fig, hoping it would keep her young and beautiful forever. But Pingala was obsessed with a horse-membered groom in the king's stable, and gave the fig to him, thinking it would improve his stamina. The groom, in turn, was shtupping a prostitute, and he gave the magical fig to her. The prostitute, being a loyal subject, and perhaps the tale's true hero, requested an audience with the king, and handed the fig to her monarch, wishing him long life.

King Bhartrihari recognised the fig (by now a bit manky), and put two and two together. Realising that his beloved Pingala had betrayed him, he opened his mouth and popped the fig in. It tasted squishy, mushy, flyblown, rotten, with subtle overtones of yeast, papilloma and horse dung. But the fig worked as promised: the king did indeed live an extraordinarily long time.

Following his disappointment, Bhartrihari's personality changed completely. He detached himself from material splendour and earthly possessions, leaving his palace, divesting himself of his power, and living out his remaining decades (all twenty of them) in a small hut in the forest. He bathed each morning in a cascading waterfall, spoke to no-one but the deer, and wrote his masterpiece, *The Three Shatakas*.

Oh, but wait! Before I go into the erotic and moral beauty of the shatakas I need to tell you how I discovered both the poetry and the shruti box. It was in the closest thing Summerville has to an Indian restaurant, Belles House of Pizza in Palmetto Plaza, a run-down mall out along Bacons Bridge Road. Actually, there's nothing Indian about Belles; it's run by a Lebanese couple who tell people they're Greek-Americans, and offers substandard pseudo-Italian food. But if you ask to use the toilet you may, as I did, hear the faint sound of Indian music throbbing through a light ply partition.

Following the sound, oblivious now to your bladder or bowels, you may well push aside a number of dry-cleaned dresses still in their plastic wrappings and discover a concealed staircase that leads—you discover, descending step by step in pulsing red light—to a cellar in which a small group of Indian men are gathered around a chanting figure dressed entirely in white.

If you're anything like me, you will now apologise for your intrusion but be greeted with warmth and entreated to join the gathering. Unable to resist such exoticism and hospitality, and completely forgetting your dinner partners upstairs, you will stay there for many hours, inhaling deeply from the bubble pipe being passed around and feeling your cultural particularity melting into the haze.

We return many times to that room, don't we, dear reader? We befriend Pranay and Ritesh and Vimal and Anish. We learn Sanskrit, purchase *The Three Shatakas*, and the shruti box. We take great pleasure in reading the erotic verses aloud, pumping the shruti, and puffing the pipe. And then, late one night, we are interrupted by the aforementioned scream. We discover that the elderly handyman Jack Brandt has an illegal family of Nicaraguan immigrants living in his glass-walled utilities room, hidden behind an artfully-arranged jungle of mops, dusters and buckets.

It's unclear quite how many of them there are, but because no official record of them exists, Brandt is free to subject them to his regime of terror. He has killed a few, that seems certain. The scream betokens fresh slaughter, perhaps. But it's best not to get involved in domestic disputes. King Bhartrihari has taught you that. Given the choice of love and hate, choose love, he says.

And so you return to your candle-lit room, narrowly avoiding Dolorosa Mendoza, who rotates silently beside a promotion for aerosol foot deodorants. "Like a tennis ball served by a dervish", I would tell you, if similes were my thing.

16

Today I've been asked to meet a representative from Adidas. His name is Karl Heinrich, and he has flown specially from Europe to talk to us about a new range of sweat-eating shoes.

While I wait for Karl's car to arrive from the airport, I read a gripping passage in Colin Wilson's book *Supernatural*. Wilson describes how the British poet Richard Church, as a young lad in a convalescent home, discovered that he could fly.

The young Church experiences an epiphany: spying a distant woodman lopping dead branches off a tree, he realises that the sound of the blows reaches him after the sight of the axe hitting the wood. From this Church infers that the laws of the universe are flexible. If time and space are lies, why not gravity?

"The drag of the earth was my most hated foe", Church writes in his autobiography. "It would pull me day and night, making every movement, even the smooth gestures which we throw in sleep, a labour too heavy to be borne; the putting on of clothes, the passage from chair to chair, the endless travel from one room to another...

"Still conscious of the warm blood whispering in my veins, I looked down at my wrist and saw the transparent flesh, the bird-bones, the channels of blue beneath the skin. All this was substance as fragile as a plant. It could not possibly outweigh the solid earth under my feet, where I and the rest of duped mankind walked with such docility."

Duped mankind!

"The sun had brightened to a liquid fire that dazzled my sight,
reducing the woodman and his brief moment of revelation
to a penumbral figure under the shadow of the bushes in the
dead grey frost. I stared at the light, and the stuff of life within
my body began to increase its speed of flow. I sensed, with a
benignancy deeper and more assured than reason, that my
limbs and trunk were lighter than they seemed, and that I had
only to reduce them by an act of will, perhaps by a mere change
of physical mechanics, to command them off the ground; out
of the tyranny of gravitation."

He had only to reduce the weight of limbs and trunk to float
off the ground!

"I exerted that will, visualising my hands and feet pressing
downwards upon the centre of the earth. It was no surprise
to me that I left the ground, and glided about the room (which
was empty) some twelve or eighteen inches above the parquet
floor. At first I was afraid of collapsing, of tumbling and
hurting myself. But I had only to draw in a deep breath, and
to command the air through the heavy portions of my
anatomy, watching it flow and dilute the solid bone and flesh
through the helpful chemistry of the blood, this new, released
and knowledgeable blood, and I soared higher, half-way to the
ceiling. This thoroughly frightened me, and I allowed myself to
subside, coming to ground with a gentleness that was itself a
sensuous delight."

He left the ground and glided about the room! And, as Colin
Wilson is at pains to point out, this is not a metaphor but a
report of something which actually happened!

I close the book, intent on trying the technique. To my surprise,
it works. Soon I am hovering quite happily in the air, learning

how to change angle and attitude by flapping my hands and tilting my weight. It's very liberating. Suddenly there's a lot more space in the store. I explore the light and airy places above the atrium, and find a good platform for my meeting with Karl Heinrich.

From my aerie I spy Karl rambling around the sales court, photographing the displays, a rucksack on his back. Landing nimbly a step behind him, I surprise the German.

"Karl, great to meet you!"

Karl twists around, surprised, and we shake hands. His English is pretty good, but queer sibilants give him away.

I am determined to test my hunch that other people, given an initial leap of faith, could fly too.

"Karl, I want you to work with me here. There's a meeting space up in the atrium, but we need to fly there. Let me show you how."

I instruct Karl in the basic movements. An enthusiastic learner, he has soon mastered the leap, the flap, the parry, the flip, the dodge, the landing.

Soon we are hovering above acres of tiny clothes rails, clearing the tops of soaring display units. We rise at about the speed of an escalator.

I look at Karl, and he grins back. Down below, Willy is waving at us.

"Now I see why they call you Brad *Power*", remarks Karl. "You are for sure releasing the unknown potentials!"

"Put it down to kryptonite and malicious animal magnetism", I smile.

At the western end of the warehouse a climbing wall has been installed. Colourful bolt-grips pepper irregularly-angled planes of concrete. Some teenaged mountaineers turn on precarious crampons to wave.

We alight on the platform atop the atrium, and Karl begins to unpack video projection equipment from his briefcase. Fortunately there is a power outlet nearby.

We sit cross-legged on the floor and Karl shows me a four-minute movie about the SweatSuck range. It has been very professionally filmed. Beautiful young runners are trying to escape from historic East Germany early on a foggy morning. We see them sprinting up to a barbed-wire fence, then suddenly leaping over it in slow motion.

Next the athletes must cross No-Man's Land, dodging vicious guards. Machine guns explode into life, but the white fire fails to touch our muscular heroes, who now leap over a second fence and are welcomed into the Land of Liberty by cheering crowds.

The final scene is a close examination of the shoes: not a single speck of blood, sweat, mud, semen or tears can be seen. Nor do the shoes smell, as we can see from the shining faces of the well-heeled capitalist dogs sniffing them.

"Applause!" I declare when the film finishes. "That's a well-realised promotion, Karl!"

"Thank you, Brad. In fact I directed it myself!"

It turns out that Karl has ambitions to become a professional filmmaker. He intends to spend some of his business trip making a documentary here in Summerville about people who have caused fatal traffic accidents by texting while driving. He hopes to sell the film to a responsible phone company.

Karl has researched his topic impressively. He recounts a horrific accident in which a commercial van-driver, texting a sarcastic comment about Lady Gaga, ploughed into a horse and buggy, killing an entire Amish family. He adds that the Amish are descended from Germans from his own ancestral seat, the Rhinish town of Bad Krozingen.

"It's certainly a long way to have come just to be killed by Lady Gaga", I say, perhaps tactlessly. As I speak it occurs to me that Karl may himself be an Amish disguised as a modern businessman.

Karl takes the comment in his stride. "Did you know that Lady Gaga has Italian roots?" he asks.

"I did not", I reply, rising to my feet and flexing my hands. "Karl, we'll take the entire SweatSuck range. It has been a pleasure to meet you, and good luck with your documentary!"

We execute the secret handshake and go our separate ways; me up towards the precarious service gantry I have recently been using for naked calisthenics and Karl down to the car park, where his buggy awaits.

17

I often pause in front of the staff photograph displayed in the entrance lobby. It looks like an illustrated edition of the *Character Sketches of Theophrastus*.

Here we all are, dressed in matching red shirts and black ties, with name and official job title displayed below in white letters on a blue background. All that's missing are the thumbnail sketches that served Menander so well when he came to write his comedies.

Hmm, "Preciosa Mendoza, Accountant". Who would she be in Theophrastus's schema? Perhaps the Garrulous. Given half a chance, Preciosa will tell you about the dream she had last night, overshare the defects of her husband, and anticipate the year's religious festivals one by one, informing you cheerfully (which you already know, of course) that the Metageitnia honours Apollo, and that during Pyanepsion it's the turn of the festival of Apaturia, when young Athenians are readied for marriage by way of initiation rituals.

I would be the Plausible: "His house abounds with rarities, he is skillfull in training apes and monkeys, he keeps Sicilian doves, he cannot play at dice unless they are carved from the finest buck's horn, he displays curiously-turned crewets, his walking-stick is a twisted Spartan staff, his rooms are hung with figured tapestries of Persia, he has a court always prepared for wrestling, and adjoining it a billiard room."

Willy would be the Vain: "When his son is of age, instead of a private festival among his friends, usual on such occasions, he makes a solemn journey with him to Delphos, to consecrate the honours of his shorn head to Apollo. He takes vast pains to be provided with a black servant, who always attends him in public. If he has a considerable sum of money, he provides himself with new coin for the purpose. If he has joined in a cavalcade, he sends his servant home with his horse and trappings; but he retains the robe of ceremony, with which he stalks about in the forum during the rest of the day. Having dedicated a brazen coronet to Esculpius, he encumbers it with chaplets."

Old Jack Brandt, the handyman, would be Asclepius, the god of medicine and healing. His daughters are in fact Hygieia, goddess of hygiene and sanitation; Iaso, the goddess of recuperation from illness; Aceso, goddess of healing process; Aglæa, goddess of beauty and adornment; and Panacea, goddess of universal remedy.

Oh, wait, Asclepius isn't one of Theophrastus' characters!

18

Poseideon has made way for the snows of Gamelion. The glaucous larkspur, dichotomous and leafy, is nowhere to be seen. Zeus inhabits Amphitryon's body to seduce a man's wife.

I've been sent home in disgrace after a pair of ice skates I customised caused multiple deaths at the Stardust Skate Center in North Charleston. It's the ideal opportunity to show you around my house. I'll fill you in on some of the details of the Stardust tragedy as we go along.

Let's start in the basement. Mind, the stairs are very steep! I'll just switch on the strip lights. Okay. Now, this place has an interesting origin. The reason I got it so cheap is that the building was somewhat notorious.

The house was built in 1974 by a serial killer, Mike Chicago. He constructed it with his bare hands. He turned the basement into a cold store in which he could hang the corpses of his victims like coats in a closet. There were thirty-five of them in here when Chicago was at the peak of his game. One of them was the feminist artist Judy Chicago (no relation).

Following the lead of "The Summerville Cannibal", I've kept the basement cool enough for meat to stay fresh and edible. I do keep some sides of venison down here, some loins of pork, a few pepperoni pizzas. But I've also installed an indoor rink. I love to skate. I think Mike would have loved it, too, if he hadn't gone over to the dark side.

When Willy took delivery of a sample pair of Riedell Gold Medallions, I jumped at the chance to put them through their paces. It was a weekend. Willy was all set to give the skates to his nephew, Billy, but when I told him about my home rink he tossed the box my way, asking for a report first thing Monday.

While freestyle figure-skating on Saturday morning—I was improvising a dance in memory of Mike's victims, whose spirits have become a sort of invisible audience for me, a kind of gallery I play to when I'm alone—I discovered that the skate blades needed a tad more bite.

Fortunately, Mike left a precision knife-sharpening machine which the police failed to seize during their investigation, a Gockel RB3. That, if you know your knife-grinders, is a top-notch piece of German kit used in wholesale butchery.

Tipping my hat to Mike's memory (he died on board a ship as it was passing through the Red Sea), I inserted the Riedells into the Gockel. The result was incredible. Speed and smoothness increased fivefold. Metal, glue, plastic and leather all flexed beyond the manufacturer's intended tolerances. Subtle, supple movements were possible, and all with perfect balance. My audience of victim spirits raised a unanimous set of tens.

The cold is quite something, isn't it? Let's go back upstairs; I'll lock up here. Okay, so, through this door. Now, this part of the house features Portugese tiles. The patterns have a Moorish origin; Islam developed its mastery of abstraction because representations of the human and the divine were forbidden. I visited Portugal in 2006 and was impressed by the bright, reverberant interiors, beautiful yet easy to clean. I had these tiles shipped in from a ceramics factory in Porto. It was cheaper than buying a job-lot of nothing-tiles at Lowe's.

Okay, before we move on to the next room I should address the tragedy at Charleston. While it's true I did go there to show off my new skates and the neat moves they facilitated, I strongly object to the sequence of events portrayed in police and media accounts. Sure, I may have slipped at one point; I'm not perfect. Yes, there may then have been a human pile-up during which six adolescents, their throats tender and bared, may have made contact, one after the other, with the sharpened blades of the Gockel-adapted Riedells.

But I am no fan of slasher movies. I guarantee that—had my eyes not been full of young blood—I would have made every effort to avoid major arteries. I was as shocked as everyone else when I saw those corpses, so young, so beautiful in their own way—their expressions surprisingly tranquil, their complexions pallid and waxy, as if a skilled undertaker had already been at work—strewn across the ice like mangled umbrellas or crashed flamingos. My first thought was: "Oh my God, Killer Mike strikes again!"

While Chicago must certainly bear some of the blame post-humously (it was, after all, his Gockel), I believe my lawyer was correct to point out that the teenagers were tailgating me, tempting fate. He also argued that the ice at the Stardust was in a near-lethal condition, and called on expert witnesses to rip apart the Stardust maintenance crew.

Finally, some blame has to be apportioned to the Fates, the Furies, the Augurs and the Chorus, who saw all this coming, in some instances specifically laying the groundwork, in others intoning details in a low hum.

That point comes from Euripides, not my lawyer.

By the way, this is my bedroom. The floor tilts. That's deliberate. I got the idea from some loft-dwelling bohemians in Hamburg who made their place look like the galleys of a clipper ship. I always like to joke that whereas the Beatles came back from Hamburg with pillock hairdos, I returned with hammocks and pillows.

So, as I was saying, although I was fully exculpated over the skate-blade business, Willy felt the need to make some kind of public gesture of distance. So he asked me to take a few days off just to appear to be thinking about my misdemeanours, then come back fresh on Thursday.

Let's end in the kitchen. I've tried to create the type of kitchen a Berlin artist would have, with some invites to shows at Contemporary Fine Arts, some spare communist chairs from the Boxhagenerplatz market, a really good cafetière and a poster with a John Baldessari quote on it.

Mine says: "I will not make any more boring art." It's my tribute to Judy Chicago.

19

It is still Gamelion. The fairy spud extends from the herbaceous border a set of frightening nectariferous claws.

My days of ease and leisure are over; Willy has appointed a team of consultants to maximise efficiency in the store.

The sly fop did it without telling anyone, so when Chuck Atkins and his three "enablers" arrive I'm sunbathing up on the atrium platform. I say "sunbathing"; in fact, I've been suffering from photophobia recently, so I've covered the glass skylight with garbage bags scotch-taped into place. It makes for a cubbyhole of perfect obscurity.

So I'm lying here listening to an album of electronic Afropop by Francis Bebey, a Cameroonian writer who lived in Paris and worked for UNESCO. I'm twitching and flexing to a seven-minute epic called "Agatha" when Willy barks my name over the intercom. I'm forced to float sheepishly down to earth, elbowing granules of sleep from my eyes and pulling my tie straight.

"Does this employee have permission to float like that?" demands Atkins before he even asks my name.

I extend a hand. "Brad Power, pleased to meet you."

Atkins barely grunts his own name back. This is not going to be a particularly chivalric relationship.

"What's your favourite animal?" snaps Atkins. I'm taken by surprise. Better not say sloth.

"I don't know, perhaps a lemur?"

"And why would that be?"

"I guess I like the idea of living at night in a tree in Madagascar, and being able to see everything that's happening around me with enormous eyes."

Atkins makes a face that seems to say "fruit cake".

"I draw the line at eating bugs, though", I add, just in case Atkins plans to put me on a new diet.

"The reason I ask", explains the consultant slowly, "is that I am trying to connect all employees in this establishment with their shamanic companion animals. I believe the store's full potential will not be met until everyone knows which spirit animals stalk them in the netherworld."

Now it's my turn to make the "fruit cake" face.

"Shamanic companion animals? That's very interesting", I say. "I never heard of that."

"Well, you're going to hear a lot more about it, so stay tuned", says Atkins, and Willy nods. The five of them march off to the accounts office, presumably to ask Mrs Mendoza the animal question, too.

Over the next few days Atkins starts referring to us all by our animal names. I'm "Lemur". Mrs Mendoza is "Skunk" (I think she was joking, but they made her stick with her first choice). Brandt the handyman is "Boar". Willy is "Rhinoceros". Chuck

Atkins himself is "Stag", and his three enforcers are "the Chipmunks". Even dead Randy Lee is retrofitted with an animal name: "Panda".

I soon begin to regret choosing a small, self-deprecating animal. Apparently this shamanic thing only works if we take on the characteristics of the beasts we're named after. The rhino, boar and stag all have jabbing horns or tusks, but the poor old lemur just sits there, regarding the forest in a drugged, bewildered sort of way. This becomes my fate.

At first it's not so bad. I'm sent back up to my hideaway, high in the forest canopy. A sort of lookout, I'm charged with alerting the other animals when I see humans (customers) approaching. The others scamper about on the sales court, mostly involved in territorial marking, mating displays, spoor deposits, visits to the water hole and the occasional burst of ceremonial violence. The skunk, hated by all, lurks in her office.

But soon we're so much in role that we're eating foods associated with our companion animals. Atkins the Stag insists that lemurs eat insects, and brings me a bag of disgusting cockroaches. But I contradict him: larger lemurs, of which I am clearly one, are frugivores by preference, and omnivores only when starving. So I will eat fruit purchased from the local farmer's market. It's a narrow escape, and Atkins the Stag leaves the cockroaches with me.

The next development is that we are asked to enter our roles via a shamanic trance.

"Brad the Lemur, watch this!" cries Atkins the Stag, clad in a shapeless fur dress and banging a tambour with a detached antler. He starts huffing and puffing and swearing and chanting in rhythm with the drum beats. Then he falls masturbating to the floor, foam flecking his distinctively cleft artiodactyl lips.

While Atkins the Stag writhes around, his lieutenants the Chipmunks start to twitter and tweep.

"Now do what he's doing! Now do what he's doing!" they chirrup.

Jesus Christ, it's totally undignified! But I get down there on the floor and start intoning made-up words:

LEEMY-POOPY-DANKY-DONKY-DOO!

Um, what else?

MADA-GAAAAR, MADA-GEEEER, MADA-GASKAR, ALASKA!

Now the incoherent foamy bit:

BUBBBBABUBBBABUBBBA! SSHHHHHHHOOOOO!

I even make a few self-touches, mostly symbolic. I generally try to avoid wanking at work.

Okay, now there's a reasonable expectation that I'm a lemur for real.

But apparently not: I haven't put on my lemur costume. I didn't know I had one, but the three enforcer-chipmunks are holding it out, a stupid little padded fur coat to which a three-foot-long striped tail has been stitched.

"That's it", I shout, "I QUIT!"

QUITTYSHITTYBATTYMITTYMOO!

The animals follow me to the door, braying, baying and barking, but I won't brook any contradiction. I'm out of here.

A car pulls up alongside me. Inside is an all-American family.

"Say, do they all sell tents in there?"

I'm not quite sure how to answer.

"Uh, they do. But they're all… animals."

20

Now that I've quit my job I can listen in peace to my favourite album, *African Electronic Music 1975-1982* by Francis Bebey. I still love that Agatha track; drum machines click with tiny rim-shots, a highlife guitar bounces in the right channel, a dirty hi-hat splashes in the left, a synth plays a series of descending hook lines which seem to bounce in a cat's cradle supplied by the bubbly guitar. Over this a man's voice speaks in French. I have no idea what he's saying. The synth starts whining and gliding; the man starts laughing. He's speaking to Agatha, presumably. Now comes the chorus: *"Agatha, ne me ment pas!"*

One reason I like the song is that it reminds me of an adventure I had with a married woman of the same name I met in the shoe department at Willy's a year ago.

Agatha Moudio called me over to where she was trying on running shoes. Although it wasn't really my job, I must admit my pulse quickened as I knelt down in front of her and, fixing her big brown eyes with mine, gripped her honey-coloured ankle and eased the soft, supple shoe over the ball of her heel.

Agatha didn't take the shoes, but she did take my address. A couple of days later I saw the same big warm brown eyes gazing through my screen door. A couple of drinks later, Agatha and I had taken each other.

It was a brief affair; Agatha soon confessed that she was married. After that we lost touch, although I did keep a note of her address.

Tonight I don't want to go straight home. I'm filled with a sense of vague excitement and possibility. I decide to find out what Agatha has been up to.

I walk—like Harry Dean Stanton in *Paris, Texas*—as the crow flies, directly across country. The azaleas are in full flower at Monck's Corner.

Here's the house! It's a smart little colonnaded bungalow in a landscaped site protected by a screen of tall pines. Concrete paths twist romantically through a herb garden.

Hopping over the low mesh fence, I approach the house through a small bamboo forest which gives way to some fuzzy-headed pampas grass. I'm halted by the sound of voices. Two people—a black man and woman—are arguing on the porch.

"You lied to me!" reproaches the man. "How could you do that, lie to your husband?"

"The child is yours, Paul!" says the woman, whom I instantly recognise as Agatha.

"Don't be stupid, woman, everyone can see it's not mine!" says Paul. "The child is white! You made a white baby!"

Agatha is adamant. "He's just not adjusted yet. It takes a while for a baby to soak up the local colour."

"Soak up the local colour? How can you come and tell me nonsense like that! You're black, I'm black, this child is white! Do you think I'm crazy? Do you think I'm blind? You made him with that lover man of yours from Willy's Sporting Goods!"

I take a step back, hoping the hairy pampas grass will hide me.

Paul is affronted, confrontational: "This baby has had three months to soak up the local colour and he's still white! Is it the son of God, Agatha? Are you the Virgin Mary? Am I Joseph the Carpenter? My mother was right when she said: 'That girl will make all colour a' baby!' "

"So you won't raise a child because you say he's not your own, just because of the colour of his skin? I call that selfish and racist, downright selfish and racist!" says Agatha.

"It's a perfectly natural reaction", roars Paul, laughing scornfully. "Consider yourself lucky! You know why? Huh? Huh? Because God spoke to me in a dream and told me that I should raise this child like my own, even though it's OBVIOUS he's not mine!"

"So God told you that, did he?"

"Yes, and do you know what God said to me? He said 'Paul', he said, 'no matter whether a child is green or red or pink or blue or purple or yellow, a child is still a child, and a father is still a father'. So you're lucky, Agatha, I will raise this white child as if it were mine. Now, pour me out some more Johncrow Batty. That's the very least you can do."

I retreat cautiously, wincing at every dry stick, every whiplash branch.

"My mother was right", the man is repeating, now laughing heartily, "she said to me 'Paul', she said, 'That girl is trouble! That girl will make all colour a' baby!' "

This has all come as quite a shock to me. To summarise: It seems I have a son. I don't know his name. Another man is bringing him up. He is doing this despite knowing the child is mine. For the time being, he will not harm the child, because

God has told him not to. But who knows what will happen to my child in the future, in that precarious situation?

Pressing play on the Francis Bebey record again, I push the white buds into my ears and head back to Summerville across country, feeling like Harry Dean Stanton.

21

Can it really be Anthesterion already? The flowers of the tulip tree, solitary and terminal, are not yet to be seen.

My time since leaving Willy's has been a kind of "lost weekend". I'm not proud of everything that's happened. I'm still not quite sure how I feel about the fact that my sister Gertli came to visit, and that we had an affair.

There had always been tempestuous, incestuous currents swelling just below the surface of our relationship, but now—after many years of cathectic sublimation—they became explicit. We made love almost constantly in a room filled with plaster statuettes and potted palms, lit night and day by oil lamps draped with pink silk.

If Gertli was initially concerned that I might have been drifting into a depression after quitting my job, and was also perhaps looking for a pretext to flee her stolid, bourgeois Charleston husband and their three children and head off to a new town to become the sculptress she had always dreamed of being, it was also unbridled lust that drove her into my arms, a lust she could only now, at the age of 33, begin to acknowledge and express.

For Gertli had been seeing a psychoanalyst who had flung open the doors on her most taboo wishes.

One day Gertli had been doing word association with Dr Oovepensky. In amongst a long list of indifferent words ("black-bird", "chalk", "dispensary") Dr Oovepensky had suddenly inserted "copulation", and Gertli just as suddenly responded: "Brad! Oh my God, *Brad!*"

The revelation struck the pair of them like twin thunderbolts: all her life Gertli had been suppressing a sexual longing for her brother. And all his professional career Dr Oovepensky had hoped to stumble across a case history involving incest.

So it was with Jacob Oovepensky's full permission and endorsement that Gertli left her husband and four (did I say three?) children the very next day and travelled the 25 miles to Summerville, promising as she departed to send lurid and florid letters back to the big city detailing all her exploits. For Dr Oovepensky was, in a manner of speaking, the Dr Watson to his own Sherlock Holmes, and—professional discretion and reasonable expectations of patient privacy aside—he delighted in publishing every detail of his most salacious and sensational cases.

Gertli's children—my own five nephews and nieces—were soon forgotten in the silky boudoir where our lovemaking continued at all hours of the night and day, causing the street outside to ring loudly with the sound of Gertli's deep, throaty cries and scandalising all the stuffed shirts and clay feet of respectable Summerville society. In August the newsletter of the Dorchester Presbyterian Church even went so far as to depict us nude, gilded and interlaced on its cover, above the caption: "Daphnis and Chloe: Must we tolerate incest in Summerville?"

Gertli had certainly changed since, as babes, we'd bathed together, innocent as shepherds. Her breasts had grown to a massive size, for one thing, and the nipples were like ripe rosy apples, tweaked by the insistent gums of six successive babies. I, on the other hand, had only grown thinner. Now, when she bounced on top of me, Gertli almost crushed me.

Soon Dr Oovepensky began to attend our sessions, sitting at the foot of the bed with an iPad and bluetooth keyboard, like Dr Watson with his service revolver. Sometimes he would mumble aloud when writing, and we would hear disembodied phrases from his account as it took shape:

"Two siamese twins who, after successful separation, can overcome overwhelming anxiety only by re-conjoining as frequently and as passionately as possible…"

"With the force of a disengaged steam engine, speeding billiard balls, or a blocked cannon…"

"Her maternal urges overwhelmed by formerly-repressed libidinal impulses, this mother's torso twists like a gorgon on satin, gripped by appetites so long neglected…"

"Apparently oblivious to her seven children…"

It was I—mentally, physically and emotionally exhausted—who crumbled first.

"Gertli, I think you should go back to your eight children", I told her one day.

"Brad, make love to me now, here, passionately, forcefully, in my sleep!"

"But Gertli, you aren't sleeping!"

"I can sleep when I'm dead, Brad! For now, we must listen to our desires!"

"What you need to listen to, Gertli, is the pitiful cries of the nine children you have abandoned in Charleston! I can hear them now, ten little voices, like eleven kittens in a barrel, being held under water, their twenty-four tiny lungs filling even as they splutter out your name! Can you really countenance thirteen deaths? Is your lust so much more important than fourteen lives?"

At last—as if by some rhetorical arithmetic—these escalating pleas began to work on Gertli. Packing her gigantic breasts into one bra, and the rest of her luggage into another, she made for the door, turning only to say to me, her eyes streaming with tears:

"I am going back to my fifteen dear little ones in Charleston, Brad. I have weighed the continued existence of sixteen souls against my passion for my own brother, and the seventeen have won. Here I come, my precious eighteen!"

And with that she returned to her nineteen children, all twenty of them.

22

Once upon a time, if you were fired, you spent the day watching the soaps on daytime television. This drove you crazy, and you were soon desperate to get back into the labour market.

Now, though, there's the internet. You can fill the screen with whatever you want. For instance, I was just watching a video of a snake whose head had been cut off. A decapitated snake's head can stay alive for up to an hour after being cut off, and this creature had decided to spend that hour attacking its own body, which was still writhing around and occasionally dealing the chopped-off head accidental blows. So the dying head ends up clamped to the twitching tail. It's viral, and hideous: you laugh, and you shudder.

Something about the scene makes me feel a bit sick. Maybe it reminds me of my current plight, cut off from employment, and therefore from respectable society. I need to look at something else.

I remember that one surefire way of feeling better about your circumstances is to gaze into the lives of people even less fortunate. Now, where's a really shitty place? I know, Trench Town, Kingston, Jamaica! So I watch a documentary about how gunshots ring out there morning, noon and night as rival gangs battle pointlessly for territory, mowing down schoolchildren and grandmothers, and killing random passersby for fun.

This works for a while—Summerville is paradise in comparison!—but it begins to make me feel gloomy about human nature in general. So I click a link for a video of an old reggae song by The Congos:

Row, fisherman, row
Keep on rowing your boat!
Lots of hungry-belly pickney they ashore
Millions of them!

I have no idea what a pickney is, but those folks are hungry, damn it, and on the boat we've got "wenchman, sprat and mackaba"! Help is on the way, pickney millions!

I like this atmosphere. It reminds me of the Salt Life.

I click another link. It's still The Congos, but now they're old men with missing teeth and concave, semi-empty eye sockets. They're snorting on gigantic bongloads of ganja and making a weird record with some hipsters who've flown in from LA.

Sun Araw is a skinny white dude with forward-combed hair and a porno stache. M. Geddes Gengras looks like a young Allen Ginsberg. He has a round face, a beard and severe 1950s spectacle frames. Some Brooklyn hipster called Tony Lowe is making a documentary about their trip to Jamaica. They've taken ten days in a studio in Portmore to put together a record with The Congos. It's Black Dice-meets-Lee Scratch Perry. Electronica-meets-Rastafarianism. Trestle-table electronica married to Biblical themes. American hipsters crossed with Jamaican Rastamen.

We don't have guys like Sun Araw in Summerville. He's originally from Austin, Texas, but now he lives in Long Beach, California. His real name is Cameron Stallones. If a skinny art-guy like that appeared in Summerville, he'd get beaten up for being "gay".

Now I'm on Pitchfork's YouTube channel. They have a clip of Tony Lowe's documentary. It all looks impossibly cool. A voice shouts "Jah Rastafari!" but instead of a trad reggae track there's this burbling weird psych-electronica under shots of herons wading in the sea and the pickney millions carrying their bright plastic billycans. Meanwhile Sun Araw sits under the ragged eaves of a tumbledown shack filling his lungs with draw from a black rubber tube which leads to a small bottle. Then there's a cute black puppy falling down on the sand in slow motion, repeatedly, like Lowe is high while editing it.

The sun is shining in Portmore. There's a swimming pool that looks like a paddy field. We pan across incandescent skeletal lightbulbs while strange liquid noises merge with burbling synth notes. A tambour thumps, but it's nothing like a regular rhythm. More shots of the old black men taking huge weed hits.

Lowe explains that Cam and Ged brought six or seven rhythms down with them and played them to the doped-up sexagenarians in the studio "super-nervously".

"Everyone was so curious about what was going to go down, like, who these guys were, coming down to do this thing?"

For me, the highlight of the clip is a painted lion on the studio wall. The contrast! There's all the technical gear of a regular recording studio: booms and mics and pop screens and cables. And then, behind it, there's this religious symbol, the Lion of Judah, looking on with his friendly, dopey-but-dignified face, and it's painted in this basic, artless, primitive style, like one of Misaki Kawai's *heta uma* (or "deliberately bad") animal paintings.

The childish sincerity really wins you over. I mean, who needs a realistic-looking Lion of Judah, right?

My reverie is interrupted by a text message. It's God, telling me that my son is named Abraham.

23

I am in someone else's room. I don't know how I got here.

The room has certain marked characteristics. There are six different styles at play here, all used in an ironic way. The styles are: classical, hi-tech, brut, rococo, Dutch, rustic. A green undulating hyperbolic paraboloid is being projected onto the white wall. The other walls are chromium yellow, ultramarine, mustard and chocolate brown.

The room's owner is not here. Perhaps I am the rightful owner of the room, since I am here and the owner is not? Perhaps it is just a matter of staying here long enough to establish de facto ownership?

And at once my brain begins to whirr with schemes. I will argue that there was no original owner of this room. After all, proof that a person has been removed from this place is missing, along with the person.

To be entirely satisfied that this room did in fact belong to someone else, I would need the missing person to give me an eyewitness account of his own removal. Since he is missing, he cannot offer that.

The situation is this: either there was no person here, in which case no person can offer a firsthand account of having lived here before me, or there was a person here who subsequently went missing, and therefore cannot meet my criteria for proving he was here, which is the testimony of a firsthand witness. In both cases I will be forced to conclude that I am the first occupant of this white, yellow, ultramarine, mustard and brown space.

Either there was a person here, or there was not, but in either case there was not a person here, according to my criteria. Of course it is entirely possible that according to the missing person's own criteria, she was indeed here. But these criteria are unknowable to me, and largely irrelevant.

I have been trying to put a brave and defiant face on it, but there is something frightening about being here alone, in this room with its green undulating hyperbolic paraboloid, in this state of considerable uncertainty.

It is possible that I will be punished for being in this room. The people who once loved me will hate me, because I came into this room uninvited, replacing the rightful occupant, whose existence is almost inconceivable to me.

It's true that I do remember rumours that coming into this room would not be the right thing to do. I must have forgotten this advice at my moment of entry, or set it aside. It's not that coming in here was forbidden. But I was led to believe that nice people did not enter such a room, or rather that one ought not even to want to enter rooms like this. If one were caught wanting to enter a room like this, one would let everybody down. It would be the beginning of the end of one's credibility. Supplies of tolerance and patience with one's waywardness would start wearing out quickly. All the freedoms one took for granted would begin to be marked as privileges which could be revoked at any moment.

There was a moment, just after mistakenly entering the white, yellow, ultramarine, mustard and chocolate room, when I could have left it with my reputation intact. But now it's too late.

Nobody who knows the amount of time I have been sitting here would accept that I made every reasonable effort to leave, or that I do not in fact desire to sit here and perhaps eventually occupy the room.

By dwelling here for the amount of time I have, I have assented to the protection the room offers from the elements. The walls of the room prevented my escape, but now the room is telling me that I could have escaped had I really wished. The fact that I did not means I welcome all that may now befall me in the room, including all sorts of exotic punishment. But I have signed up for none of it.

I have brought the room's harsh treatment of me—should it now begin—upon myself. But I am innocent!

Society told me to leave the room alone, or else! The room—its green hyperbolic paraboloid undulating like a sinister brain—heard that, saw an advantage for itself in weakening me and began provoking me to enter it unlawfully, knowing I would be punished if I did. The room is a much more formidable adversary than I at first assumed when I violated it by entering through a window. The room has a lot up its sleeve.

But I can just walk away from this situation! Neither society nor the room can get annoyed by an absentee, surely? An absentee cannot become a scapegoat. So I will absent myself. If someone subsequently comes to the room and occupies it, they will have to infer my former presence in the room by logical deduction alone. They will conclude, probably, that only a direct account from myself will suffice to prove that I ever dwelt in this room, and that if no such account is produced, I was never here.

I am rising to leave when I hear a key in the lock. Someone is coming into the room, and not through the window! The rightful occupant! I immediately dive under the bed.

24

Into the room comes a twitchy albino mesomorph with the shaggy head of a lion. He's confined to a wheelchair.

"Good evening, Mr Power, I am Icek Judko", says the lion-headed man. "Welcome to my den!"

Apparently we're in an unmarked warehouse out on Interstate 26. Judko poses as a furniture restorer, he tells me, but his real project is to invent the crimes that unimaginative lawmakers have so far failed to forbid.

Without false modesty, Judko tells me that he's smarter than criminals, smarter than cops and smarter than lawyers. Only inventors and artists can keep up with his racing brain. So far, nothing has been pinned on him because nothing is strictly illegal about parbezzling, embroilment, stretch-and-wait, money-lingering or parallel porking.

"See this wheelchair I'm in?" demands Judko, who has pink eyes. "There's no real need for it. I could get up and walk any time. If I were walking right now I'd be nothing more than normal. Restricted like this, I have a miracle up my sleeve: the miracle of walking."

"For the normal man", continues Icek Judko, whose arms are freckled and hairless, "walking is just normal. For me it's both normal and a miracle. I have the choice. I also get better parking options and alibis."

Icek Judko's other big self-imposed restriction is ferrules. Every scheme and trick he comes up with has to use them.

Ferrules, in case you don't know, are spherical bonding clamps crimped or swaged onto elements like fibres and wires. Think of the bracelet-like bonds at the end of your shoelaces, or the metal band around the eraser atop your pencil.

I'm sitting at Icek's big round table, here in the warehouse. He's telling me about a card system he's using. This might be genuine, or it might be a ruse to see whether I'm trustworthy.

One set of ten cards, Icek explains, lists the scams he's been working recently. Another set lists ten specific types of ferrule. He shuffles randomly, then lays the cards out on the table in pairs. Now the challenge is to make each scam work in a new way with its randomly-assigned ferrule.

"How would you do it?" he asks me, powering his wheelchair out of the way and signalling me to take his place before the cards. I can't help noticing that he has no fingernails.

I'm confronted by the following pairs:

Park Lane scam / The metal ferrule that holds the horsehair in place on the frogs of violin bows.

Calypso Scheme scam / Shoelace aglet.

Parbezzling scam / Ring that bonds a chisel blade's tang to its handle.

Family Filter scam / Sleeve connecting a hypodermic needle to the plastic Luer taper leading to a syringe or intravenous tubing.

Cascading Termination scam / Plastic ferrule found on golf club shafts just above the hosel of the club head.

Embroilment scam / Compression fitting for attaching tubes to pipes, tubes to tubes or pipes to pipes.

Stretch-and-Wait scam / Cap tip for cane or umbrella.

Money-Lingering scam / Male and female joints that allow a two-piece fishing rod to snap together.

Parallel Porking scam / Swaged termination type for wire rope.

Insider Bleeding scam / The metal or plastic ring used in plumbing as part of a compression fitting along with a slip-on nut for making a liquid-tight connection when joining pipe or tubing.

I'm stumped.

"Start with the last one, that's the easiest", says Icek, who has weirdly low-hanging earlobes.

"But I know neither the general principles nor specific practises of Insider Bleeding", I protest.

"If you did, I'd have to kill you", jokes Icek, who has a bright red turkey wattle. "Good, knowing what you don't know is always the correct first step; the 'known unknowns', to quote a hero of mine. Now, let's take that logic even further. Let's look for the unknown unknowns, the things we don't even know we don't know."

I'm baffled. "What don't we know we don't know?'

"Well, you know you don't know what crimes will exist in the future", suggests Icek, who has duck lips. "You also know you don't know what I'm currently doing under the description of Insider Bleeding. So those can be eliminated. Try to guess something you don't know you don't know."

I take a wild stab.

"In the world in which I am a fish, being a fish is a crime?"

"It could be…" Icek has male-pattern baldness on his chest.

Suddenly I get a little flurry of inspiration. "There's a missing set of cards!" I exclaim.

"Yes!" says Icek. "What do they depict or represent? Think hard. We have scams, and we have ferrules. What's the third element?"

"Scams, ferrules and… Scams, ferrules and…" Nothing seems to suggest itself as a third element.

I guess wildly.

"Fish?"

"Good, good, I like that!" shouts Icek, whose halitosis has earwax. "It's not what I had in mind, but let's follow where it leads."

Spurting the power on his hand controller, he zooms up to the table and begins to scribble the names of fish on blank cards. Then he shuffles the ten cards and lays them beside the scam and ferrule combinations.

Insider Bleeding / Tube Nut / Largemouth Bass, reads the final sequence.

"Nice. I think we're really getting somewhere", says Icek Judko.

"Now, what do you know about String Theory?"

I have no idea how to answer.

"Isn't the largemouth bass the state fish of Mississippi?"

I can't help noticing that Icek Judko, nodding sagely, has dry skin.

25

O, fairest dawn that ever greeted Summerville! The sun's golden eye is ablaze on Dirce's spring! The ochre brittlegill releases clouds of spore from adnexed gills!

In the great conflict between ZZ Top and Kraftwerk, fate at first seems to smile on the Germans. The battle unfolds on the asphalt before Greenway Self-Storage on Boone Hill Road, a circuit of green garage doors protected by a low fence, a STOP sign, and a watchman's cabin.

Their white Mercedes gleaming, the Germans demolish the low fence in frenzied flight, flattening the STOP sign. Florian Schneider is at their head, remorseless in his wrath.

Into the self-storage compound they swoop like an eight-eyed eagle with wings of snow, heavy with armour, exhaust fumes streaming. Their bloodthirsty spears menace the seven garages, in each of which stands a Texan astride an idling Harley.

But, their lust unsated and all the Harleys unburned, the Germans are soon on the run from the dragon-sired soldiers of Texas. For Zeus abhors a braggart! As they storm the roller doors in brazen clamour, Zeus strikes down each man who breaches a garage. The Oldworldians are routed by the New.

At last Florian Schneider and Billy Gibbons face off, brothers turned sour with rancourous rivalry. They cross their spears and perish together.

Now in brightest victory let war be forgotten! Let our temples ring with night-long rejoicing! For Summerville is spared.

Mayor Bill Collins rises to speak.

"Welcome to Summerville, the flower town in the pines! Stimulating progress and a rich history blend to form a unique town with an exciting story to tell.

"Schneider and Gibbons are dead, each one killed by the other's hand. I swear to you by all-seeing Zeus that I will never turn away from trouble. I shall keep Summerville mighty. Hear my decree regarding these musicians!

"Only one of them, my good friend Billy Gibbons, who died a hero in our defence, shall be buried with every honour due the noble dead. The other, Florian Schneider, who came from exile raging to set fire to the city and to desecrate its altars, who strove to kill his rival and enslave us all, I forbid you to honour him even in death!

"Schneider shall lie unburied, for the dogs and vultures to pick clean. That is my command."

A ripple runs through the crowd. This is harsh.

"We are recognised as a nurturing community, where children can grow and develop. A thriving economic development focus, world-class sports venues and superior schools make Summerville a truly special place. But we shall not tolerate treachery."

As the hesitant applause dies down, Mayor Collins retires to his palace. The revels that night are unparalleled. Egged on by jubilant priests and carousing Texans quaffing wine from inverted helmets, the people of Summerville celebrate their freedom, and the hero who has ensured it.

But out at the lonely crossroads where Schneider's body has been left to rot, a mysterious figure is sprinkling ritual dust upon his naked body. It's my sister Gertli.

A burly soldier reports back to Mayor Collins that he and his companions have swept the dust from Schneider's rotting corpse and left it bare. But the stench has driven them to a nearby hillside, where they commence a gruesome watch, remaining awake by prodding each other with sharp words. Time passes, and the noonday sun scorches overhead.

Suddenly there is a whirlwind so fierce it seems the trees will be uprooted. The sky is choked with dust. The soldiers clench their eyes against the tiny storm. When it dies down they see Gertli wailing like a bird robbed of her brood, sprinkling the corpse of Schneider with sacred dust.

How wildly does the faithful Gertli curse those who stripped her hero naked! She pours out three libations of wine upon his cold skin. The men run down the hill and seize her. She shows no fear. Dragged before Mayor Collins, she confesses everything.

"You commanded that Florian Schneider's unburied body should be eaten by wild animals. But no edict of yours could ever outweigh the law ordained by the gods, that unwritten law unchanging for all eternity, its origin lost in time. Kill me now if you like, but I cannot leave my hero unburied."

Mayor Collins orders Gertli to be taken away and imprisoned. In her cell she hangs herself, and her fiancé, Haimon, upon discovering her body, chooses to die by his own hand. Mayor Colins's wife, Eurydice, on seeing the tragic outcome of the events set in motion by her husband, also kills herself by throwing her body into her enormous weaving loom while the device is in operation.

This all comes as a great shock to me. My depression is deepening significantly when suddenly I receive another text message. My son by Agatha, Abraham, is in town and wants to meet me.

26

I meet Abraham at Low Country Uniform on Ulysses S Grant Parkway. He's certainly grown up fast!

A handsome lad, Abe looks like me, only younger, more athletic, with tighter curled hair. I buy him a pair of medical orderly scrub pants, pale blue with a yellow ribbon waist cord, then we take a table at Yokoso, the Japanese steakhouse next door.

I order a Firecracker. Abraham gets a $9.99 Heartbreaker: spicy tuna and cucumber topped with albacore tuna, avocado and scallions with a drizzle of sweet ponzu sauce.

"Tuna topped with tuna?" I query.

"Yes, sir, it's a double-decker. They are taken from different areas of the fish," says the server.

To pass the time until the dishes arrive, I quiz my son about his masturbation habits.

"We've all done it, so you have too. Haven't you, Abraham?"

Abraham has no sense of sin. He tells me he gets up to all sorts of stuff to make his masturbation more interesting. For instance, he follows girls carrying a special marker pen filled with sperm instead of ink, and writes filthy messages all over their bicycles. He also likes to creep into the girls' changing room in a public swimming pool, break into their lockers, then take photographs of his penis with their cellphones.

Once, Abraham tells me, he donned a mink coat at dusk and posed as a girl's cat, allowing her to feed him milk and stroke him all curled up in her lap. At a pivotal moment he tugged off the coat to reveal his naked human body and bouncing erection.

Abraham also claims to have had his cock sniffed by all 48 members of Japanese idol group AKB48. He posed as a rare orchid and mailed himself to the Japanese idol group. The details took a bit of planning. He had to find a pot big enough to curl his whole body into, but not so big that it might arouse suspicion.

The girls check their fan mail regularly, and make a video newsletter for their website which shows every detail of the procedure, and always ends the same way: with all 48 members waving, flashing V-signs and thanking the fans for their dedication.

They were shooting one of these fan videos the day Abraham got delivered. Being the biggest present, he was kept until last. His ribbons, labels and cards were carefully snipped and set aside, his hand-decorated paper ripped off. And there he stood, one single pink orchid rising provocatively from an enormous pot.

The girls made stretchy-eye gestures and clapped their hands together. A pink flower! How gorgeous!

Of course it wasn't a flower. It was Abraham's erect penis.

Since AKB48 is an egalitarian pop group, the girls filed past to sniff my son in alphabetical order. They cooed their appreciation. Some took photographs, others suggested Latin species names, a couple took foreskin clippings, hoping to create a graft capable of flourishing in their own gardens.

Some of the girls probably recognised the "orchid" as a penis, but didn't let on. The idols are forbidden to date boys, Abraham tells me, and recognition of a penis might lead to suspension.

Their handler Etsuko did recognise my son's glans for what it was, however, and soon 48 pairs of long-nailed hands were digging his naked body out of the huge pot. Eyes were stretched again, the video was paused, and the police were called.

Abraham was hustled away to a bare cell where a hunchbacked lawyer with the face of a chimpanzee was attempting to fill out a long official form in blue biro. His white shirt smelled of perspiration. A ceiling fan spiralled overhead.

"And all 48 members sniffed it?" asked the chimp. "You could get the death penalty for this."

"Abraham", I say as my Firecracker is set down before me, "AKB48 actually has 93 members. You're a liar."

27

I think I'm having an identity crisis. Since quitting my job I have no idea where I am, who I am or what I am.

Let me try to explain this with a parable. Once there was a bird who was adopted by a dog. The bird was a dwarf bittern, *Ixobrychus sturmii*. The dog was a mongrel.

Some say the dog was jealous of the bittern's immaculate pedigree, and had decided to bully the bird to level down the social gap between them. If folk hadn't made the dog feel like it was scum, things might have been different. And if the bird had been bigger than the dog, things would certainly have been different. But so be it.

Now, the dog was known for howling whenever it heard music. This created an awful din, and the only thing which could stop it was the bittern booming. Bitterns boom during mating season; it's an eerie low-frequency sound almost inaudible to human ears, but dogs can hear it.

Did I mention that this story was taking place in Nice, on the beach? And that halfway through, rather expensively, it transferred to Zurich because the City of Nice suddenly demanded a higher filming fee?

In Zurich the dog and the bittern went to see a bank manager, who stood smiling in front of a spray of red flowers. Someone had told him that the dog was very wealthy, so he was determined to turn a blind eye to the animal's evident vulgarity. The bittern, as far as he was concerned, was of very little consequence, a trifling presence.

But halfway through the interview, the banker was handed a piece of paper. "It is the bittern which is wealthy; the dog is a mere servant!" said the note. "Servant" was underlined twice.

The banker immediately asked the bittern if it wanted its own separate chair; the bird was perched on the arm of the dog's chair.

The bittern shook its head. It was an austere bird, with a bleak perspective on life. However, it did mention to the banker that, were a plate of dried, mixed aphids to be procured, it would gladly wash them down with a small glass of water.

The banker, keen to attract the wealthy bittern's business, immediately sent two assistants out for a bowl of dried, mixed aphids. The men didn't return for nearly half an hour, by which time the banker was seething, bowing repeatedly to the bittern and apologising profusely.

But when he was handed another note, his tone rapidly changed. Now the bank manager was informed that these animals were both paupers, without a penny to their names.

The banker immediately chased the dog and the bittern out of his office, offering kicks to the backside of the trotting canine and waving his arms at the flying bird, shouting "Shoo! Shoo!"

Now, the animals had been hoping to obtain a loan which would allow them to start a newspaper in Zurich. Their newspaper would contain a very limited piece of information: the time of day. The news vendor would sell you a paper which had the time printed on it. You would be able to learn from it all the important things that had happened throughout history at precisely that moment of the day, the relevant Indian raga scales, the prayers ancient Egyptians had made at that hour, and the precautions to take in case of inclement weather. The two friends also hoped to include content of special interest to dogs and bitterns, imagining (wrongly, as it turned out) Zurich to be full of creatures like themselves.

With their dreams in ruins, the dog and the bittern went to Veltlinerkeller, a restaurant serving good plain food from a menu which included some aphid dishes. When they got there, however, the waiter informed them regretfully that all he had today was oysters.

Since both creatures disliked oysters, they went instead to the library, hoping to find a new history by Livy which, the papers said, had recently been discovered in Shangri-La after being believed lost for many centuries.

The two friends arrived just in time to see a disaster unfold: the library was burning, and several fire engines were in attendance.

"The Livy! The Livy!" shouted the librarian, and the dog, throwing caution to the wind, rushed into the inferno, seized the leather cover of the burning volume with its teeth, and saved it.

The following day the dog's portrait burnished the front of all the newspapers. DOG SAVES LIVY! sang the headlines, and GOOD DOG! CLEVER DOG! Unsure whether to be angry at the patronising tone of some of the articles, the dog nevertheless luxuriated in the praise, and made peace once and for all with the bittern: never would he utter an angry or cruel word, he swore, his eyes swimming with big doggy tears. What's more, if the bittern would stop booming, the dog would never again sing along with human music.

The two friends celebrated with a bottle of Pernod, which made them exceedingly drunk. Meanwhile, the Dictator Hall organised a speedboat celebration out on Lake Zurich; tiny boats in blue, red and yellow drew hieroglyphic outlines of the heroic animals in wake foam, visible to marine bi-planes from which bracket-mounted cine-cameras recorded everything in 70mm widescreen format.

The animals, swelling with pride and still drunk on Pernod, were carried shoulder-high by the fascist youth of Zurich.

That very evening, however, something terrible happened. The Dictator Hall was travelling in his motorcade through the Simplon Tunnel when suddenly part of the roof collapsed, squashing him and also killing several of his top generals.

Fearing that they would somehow be blamed for the disaster, the dog and the bird left the Republic of Zurich on the next available train.

In order to conceal their identities, they hid behind a copy of Ludwig Hohl's two-volume work *Notes*. The dog, wearing tinted spectacles, handed the tickets over in as casual a way as possible when the inspector passed through the carriage.

At that very moment the police were at the bank, questioning the manager about the suspicious animals. They were probably agents in disguise, he mused, sent by the rival Republic of Berne.

In Zurich people had gone mad with grief. Many men let their penises hang out of their trousers as a mark of respect. A procession of mourners carried the coffin of the Dictator Hall to the top of Clam Mountain, where his casket was ceremonially burned as an offering to the Sun God.

It then began to rain very hard indeed.

Some say the French are making the novel new again thanks to Michel Butor.

Apfelstrudel is excellent with coffee and cream.

It is four o'clock. The stuffing is coming out of the chairs. The Dictator Hall is still dead.

Dentures and the dentists who supply them have gone out of fashion. The people of Zurich eat only pancakes and panda meat.

It is a fact that almost everything is different.

The police follow the trail of clues to Ludwig Hohl's basement. Is it true that he has fired a shot through his window?

"Yes", says Hohl.

"Who were you trying to shoot?" ask the police.

"God!" Hohl replies.

"And did you get him?"

"I think so. His feet, a bit."

28

I have received a letter from God. Through the regular mail. It's quite strange. I think his mind is beginning to go.

"I am God. I am an elderly European", the letter begins.

"My hair is a thin aureole of fine coconut furze, and my beard the white fuzz upon a moulded fig. I have milk-apple cheeks unfortunately marred on the left side by a birthmark which resembles a spill of cherry juice. Hornets, wasps and bees swarm around my neck, which ancient acne (I was young once!) has scarred into the exact likeness of an African horned cucumber. My ears have the brain-shaped, yellowish arils of the ackee, known to horticulturalists as the "vegetable brain" (which is misleading, because the ackee is definitely a fruit). My eyelids are dry and delicately veined, bringing to mind the papery skin of the physalis. My eyes are twin loquats set beneath brows of jabuticaba, sometimes squirting forth sweet tears, sometimes puffs of nectar. My teeth are bitter to the taste and soft to the touch, like orange pith, and my lips two crescents of sliced lemon. Come kiss me quick, girls, if lemon juice be your bitter tipple!

"Assemble these fruits and you will have my perfect likeness. Now you cannot fail to recognise me when we pass in the orchard."

At first I think that this is the end of the letter. But then I see that God has used both sides of the paper.

"My habits are of an absolutely inviolable invariability", God continues on side two. "I begin the day at 7am with two fresh quail's eggs and a poppadom. Well, I say that, actually the day begins with harvesting the quail's eggs and making the poppadom. An extra hour is needed for these activities, so I begin the day, in fact, at 6am.

"The quail's eggs are relatively simple to harvest; I just need to crawl through a nearby forest playing on a decoy whistle the mating call of the male rufous-breasted wood quail. The females flock to me, realise they've been tricked, then return with heavy gait to their nests, leading me straight to the delicious brindled eggs.

"Well, I say 'straight to the delicious brindled eggs', but sometimes the lazy quail hens haven't laid yet, and I'm forced to wait until they do. So factor in another hour, and let's say, to be realistic, that my day actually begins at 5am. But then there's the little matter of the poppadom flour. I'm a stickler for authenticity; it must be urid flour made from dried whole black urad lentils.

"Although lentils cook quickly, there's no rushing the process of skinning and splitting them and removing the hulls. So let's say my day actually begins at 4am. But of course they must be purchased at a good price, which means my day begins, invariably, at 3am at the farmer's market.

"I say 'invariably', but I haven't factored in the time needed for the cooked lentils to cool and get mortar-and-pestled into flour, which takes at least another hour, so we're probably talking about a 2am start, realistically. Make that 1am if I am forced to source the mortar and pestle. Those things get easily lost when kids sneak into the kitchen and start playing with the utensils.

"But where the hell does one find a mortar and pestle at midnight? One is forced to make them oneself. And of course that requires clay. Luckily, clay can be made from flour. For convenience I use the same urid flour with which I make my poppadoms, mixing it in this instance with a tablespoon-full of cream of tartar. But where to find cream of tartar at 11pm?

"One is forced to create it. Potassium bitartrate (cream of tartar) is a crystalline resin made in wine casks, a by-product of the fermentation of grape juice, a process which takes at least six months. So strictly speaking my day begins (if it's July) in early February. But then there's the process of making the fire that lights the kiln that bakes the clay. It generally takes me years of fiddling around with twigs and tinder before I can get a suitable spark."

The letter is signed with the Greek symbols for alpha and omega.

29

What's the opposite of cabin fever? Agoraphobia, the fear of fields.

For the last couple of weeks I've started feeling that my house has too much space in it. It's an aesthetic feeling, a psychological state and a moral sense all wrapped up. I feel, suddenly, that my house is an outdoor space, and that I need to reestablish some indoorness.

So last weekend I made a trip out to Lowe's and bought some sheets of plyboard. Since I don't have a car, I had to bring each sheet back individually, lashed to my back with bungee cord, attachment clamps and cone hooks. It was a lot of work, but highly satisfying. I've now hammered together a tiny traditional Japanese teahouse within my living room.

The teahouse stands on slender stilts. There are four steps which must be climbed (in stockinged feet only, please!) if you want to retreat "indoors from indoors". The extra height makes the place feel like a treehouse as well as a teahouse. There isn't room inside to stand up straight, but I like that: a stooped position indicates respect. Anyway, this is not a space for standing up. This is a space for contemplation and meditation.

Why don't I have a car? It's a legitimate question for a man living in a nation where a driver's license is the default ID, and only 30% of the population has a passport.

Two years ago I had a crisis in my life. You know how I said I was super-thin? Well, I wasn't always. Quite the reverse.

Picture this: I weigh 275 pounds, I have a drinking problem, and I'm a couch potato addicted to violent video games. My favourite is *Call of Duty: Black Ops*. I play it on the Xbox 360.

What do I like about that game? I find it highly enjoyable to knife, shoot or blow people up, especially communists. I like sprinting, standing, crouching, lying prone, shooting constantly. I also like the health gauge, which has a tendency to rise over time. You'll be in the red "danger" zone, and the gauge will start slipping back into the green, like a self-filling bank account or gas tank.

I like the macho banter of my comrades, with their muscular physiques, their inability to fear anything. In quiet moments—when you're not being tortured for information, or gunning down foreigners, running together, spurring each other on with encouraging cries and back-up fire—you can kick back, suck on a Pabst, shoot the breeze about duty, freedom, family, values. "Give the other fellow hell", as McCartney put it. Yup, live and let die. Reckon that's about the size of it.

In real life, of course, quite the opposite is happening. I'm getting fatter and more effete. I'm terrified of everything. I daren't even leave the house. My car is rusting, my health deteriorating.

In Black Ops World I can be legion, playing character after character. Other agents befriend me, tell me they "got my back", risk their lives and die for me. Our government has specifically instructed us to break the law behind enemy lines, terminating the lives of communists and their leaders by extra-judicial killing. Law only applies to the weak: for the strong, law blazes from the barrel of a gun. Communism has no legitimacy. An enemy of the US can be gunned down like a dog.

In Black Ops World I have access to restricted places, I'm privy to classified information, I'm licensed to kill. I can rape, pillage, murder and raze with impunity. Black helicopters hover like cockroaches or angels, conferring the legitimacy of Realpolitik. The automatic barrels blaze, the blood of the bad spatters the lens.

When I've completed all the game's levels, it's time to face myself. I have to admit that *Call of Duty: Black Ops* has made me physically fat and mentally fascist. I sell the Xbox, sell my car, check into a clinic and submit to a liposculptural operation. Dr Ferrell removes 75% of my belly. I become the Brad I am today: slim, fit, principled, austere, eccentric.

The teahouse rests against the street-facing window of my living room, whose light is diffused through a large sheet of washi paper. Washi paper comes from the gampi tree.

30

I mentioned my affair with my sister Gertli, and her tragic fate in connection with the corpse of Florian Schneider. But I didn't mention the most important relationship in my life, which is with my mother.

Whenever I have sex now, whether with my sister or another woman, and start to enjoy the messy side, the smacking and the spattering, I always think of it as a basic attempt to recreate the conditions of my birth.

Can you remember being born? I thought not. And why can't you remember such an important experience? It's not for lack of brain; a baby has one hundred billion neurons. It's because a deeply misogynistic culture has forced you to repress the memory.

I remember my birth as if it happened yesterday. There was a loud sucking and squelching noise. My mother loosed the contents of her bowels and the odour of dung reeked out. Blood also shot up from her, and light and screams. The light and screams were all mixed up with daylight, and the red wallpaper, and my own screams, and the screams of my father and the hospital staff.

God will confirm all this, unless he's forgotten. Everyone was weeping, farting, urinating freely. The doctor gnawed through the umbilical cord, and my father gobbled down the placenta, only to burp, hiccup and vomit it up a few minutes later. For my part, I howled and pissed and struggled and only then noticed that I was breathing. The one person seemingly unconcerned was the wet nurse, who sat stirring a cauldron of onion soup, occasionally palping her bared breasts with calloused fingers so that hot milk would bubble at her nipples, ready to squirt into my greedy mouth.

This is the scene that replays in my mind every time I have messy sex, although not with my mother, despite the obvious temptation. The world would be a better place if everyone could remember their own version of this sacred scene. And the world would be a better place if due respect were rendered to that pragmatic wonder, the mother.

A mother is always the total authority in one's life, the natural authority. There is a play by Auden and Isherwood called *The Ascent of F6*. Ransom, its hero, is a mountaineer who goes to the hinterland between Sudoland and Ostnia to climb a terrifying mountain. The Ostnians, who are about to rise up against the British colonists, are a superstitious people who believe that a demon lives atop F6. They will venerate whoever climbs the mountain; whoever conquers F6, therefore, conquers them.

At the top of the mountain Ransom meets the demon, who turns out to be his mother. As he lies dying of exposure and oxygen starvation, she cradles him in her lap, sings a lullaby and feeds him a few last morsels of his favourite food: crystallised apricots.

31

I have received another letter from God.

"This is God again", it says. "At the risk of contradicting everything I said about myself before, I would just like you to know that I am, in the words of my servant Saint Denis (also known as Dionysus, the Bishop of Paris, saint and martyr), neither soul nor angel, nor do I have imagination or opinion or reason or understanding. Nor am I reason or understanding. And to pass from these high things by intermediate stages to the lowest things, I am not number, or order, or greatness, or littleness, nor am I spirit, according to your understanding of spirit, nor sonship, nor fatherhood, according to your understanding of those things, nor anything else known to you, or to any who exist. Nor am I any of the things that do not exist, nor do I know the things that exist as they are in themselves, but as they are in me.

"And that is not even a definitive process of elimination. There are many more things that I am not, and am also not not.

"After his head was chopped off, my servant Saint Denis (aka Dionysus, the Bishop of Paris) picked it up and walked ten kilometres, preaching a sermon the entire way. You can see a statue of him clutching his detached head at the Notre-Dame Cathedral. But that is by-the-by. The pressing question of the day is: Why have I commissioned you, Brad, to recreate in reverse the westward Wonder Voyage of Saint Brendan?

"The answer is that partly it's because I am bored, and simply want something interesting to happen in these pages, like someone walking and talking while headless.

"But I'm also a moralist, and it really upsets me that America has become a machine for creating unpleasant people. You don't need me to remind you of the sins of America. The gigantic eco-footprint, the far-flung military bases, the opportunistic wars, the indigenous genocide, the slavery, the guns, the nuking, the torture, the spying, the self-indulgence, the stubborn resistance to all forms of legislated social justice, the dedication to self-interest, the hypocritical claims to believe in me! Entire regions have been flooded by me for less.

"Although not much can be said of me, it is true that I like to set up situations to see what will ensue. In this case, I'd like to see if America—in her current form—can be uninvented. I'd like to subject a group of Americans, perhaps on a boat, to a process during which they become less and less American. I contemplated a series of romances on a love boat, or a *Gilligan's Island*-type comedy, or a space exploration narrative like *Star Trek*. But in the end I settled on an Irish-style Wonder Voyage.

"There will be a string of islands, each one containing an instructive adventure. I've laid it all out like a computer game, or a major world religion. Can you complete every level? Can you reach unAmerica? I promise it will be fun. It will eradicate your boredom, and perhaps mine.

"Brad, I have forgotten how to create, but not how to destroy. I have forgotten how to make metaphors, but not how to speak literally. Let me tell you a story to illustrate that.

"There's a simpleton living in Scetis who thinks that bread and wine are just symbols for the body and blood of my son. Two anchorites, hearing about this, hurry to his house and tell the simpleton that both are real and completely literal: bread really is a body, and wine really is blood. The simpleton asks for proof, and all three of them pray to me for several days.

"On Sunday the three go to church and sit down on a mat, the two anchorites flanking the simpleton. When the bread is placed on the holy table, the three men see a little child. And when the priest stretches out his hand to divide the bread into small pieces, an angel descends from heaven with a sword and pours the child's blood into a chalice.

"The priest chops the bread with a knife, but the men see the angel hacking the child into pieces. It's a gory scene, and quite difficult for me to produce. Approaching to receive the sacrament, the simpleton is handed a hunk of flesh spurting with blood.

"This grosses the simpleton out, so he screams: 'Okay, I believe you now! This bread is your flesh, and this wine is your blood! Jesus!'

"Now the dripping infant's body part in his hand turns back into bread, and the cup of blood he's holding becomes wine again.

"The anchorites explain: 'God knows that man cannot eat raw flesh. That's why he turns his body into bread and his blood into wine.'

"The simpleton still isn't satisfied. 'But why does he want to be cannibalised in the first place?' he asks, like a child.

"Brad, this is awful", concludes God, "but I've completely forgotten the answer."

32

The delightful month of Mounichion has rolled around; rhizomatous *Thalictrum* pokes its polygamous tongue across the lintel-frame.

I can't believe it's been half an Attic year since Randy Lee was murdered under his bodhi tree in Azalea Park. I think about Randy every time I pass that park, and every time I read in the paper about some terrible new act of local violence.

There's a horrific story in the *Journal Scene* today about a horse hacked to bits by a former horse-whisperer turned horse-killer. Mike Kettley murdered a steed called Parker in cold blood when it suddenly ceased responding to his whispers.

At first Kettley was content to send hate mail to the horse, which was stabled at Fair Springs on Bacons Bridge Road. "I will tamper with your paddock lock", threatened the first letter, signed "Horse-Hater". The second read: "U can galop, but U cant hide, porker!" The third simply said: "HORSE? HORE!"

Kettley knew the horse could read because he'd been the one who taught it. We tend to assume that, because they're mute, horses are dumb, but in fact they're mostly just humble. Horses are folks who keep to themselves, but they're at least as intelligent as humans, and in some cases more so.

The relationship was fine until one day Mike called Parker

"Porker" by mistake. The horse did eventually accept his urgently-whispered apologies, but by then the damage had been done. A porker is a filthy pig. A swine. No matter how the horse tried to fake it, he could no longer pretend to be charmed by Kettley's whispering. Parker would vigorously flick whichever ear Mike tried to approach, as if to dislodge a fly.

Mike got the message, and felt deeply rejected. Soon the threatening letters began, fuelled no doubt by the additional anguish of the andropause he also happened to be going through.

It all came to a head one August night when the moon was partially obscured by towering cumulonimbus clouds. Kettley's identity crisis, caused by the waning of his manhood, had made sleep increasingly difficult for him. He would sit bolt-upright in his bed, sharpening a set of Forschner Victorinox knives he'd recently purchased by mail order from Switzerland.

He'd originally sent for the knives with the idea of self-harm uppermost in his mind. But, whiling away the insomniac hours in a chatroom frequented by disgruntled butchers, he'd started to see a bigger picture. These were, after all, implements honed for professional animal butchery. They—in a manner of speaking—"longed" to be allowed to do their job.

"Forschner high-carbon stainless steel blades are hand-finished in Switzerland by skilled craftsmen. They use a special tempering process to produce an edge that can be resharpened over and over again. The handle is ergonomically designed by Victorinox to minimise wrist tension. Forschner offers over three hundred styles and types of blades suited exactly to specific functions or cutting tasks. Select the proper knife for your individual preference and need. The correct knife is a safe knife."

These are the sorts of things dark, murderous ex-butchers hiss to each other late at night while planning the perfect animal murder. Soon Kettley had gravitated to a specialist forum for the gloating of horse-murderers. Here talk was of stalking techniques, intimidation noises, knacker options, and—on a good night—the best place to plunge the blade.

"Grab HV [horse victim, in the equine murderer's argot] by crest / poll and plunge FV [Forschner Victorinox knife] into withers", advised one horse-murderer [HM], whose online handle was HM VictorX. But HM Hackjoy disagreed: "Kick HV's ergots, bind coronets, deliver jab to gaskins, plunge FV into stifle", he said. (For convenience's sake I'm talking as though men lurked behind the butchers' pseudonyms; in all fairness, these killers could also have been women.)

Kettley was known in the chatroom as HM Mikekettley. When he'd registered he hadn't been screwed up to the idea of actually murdering a horse, and hadn't thought that full anonymity would be necessary. Later, when the idea of horse-murder started becoming more attractive, he'd tried to change his details only to find that the system didn't allow it.

"Puncture throat latch with FV", suggested HM Mikekettley, "plunge second FV into fetlock, third into croup, then chop off tail."

There was a stunned silence from the forum. "CHOP OFF TAIL?" came the eventual echo, then: "LOL! Newb!"

Kettley signed out, speechless with fury, grabbed his Forschner Victorinox box, and made straight for the paddock.

Parker was discovered the next day with multiple stab wounds to the poll, forehead, muzzle, chin groove, throat latch, elbow, forearm, knee, cannon, pastern, heel, ergot, chestnut, barrel, stifle, coronet, hoof, fetlock, hock, gaskin, dock, hip point, croup, flank, loin, back, withers, shoulder and crest.

A full set of Forschner Victorinox knives was discovered near the scene of the crime, covered in Mike Kettley's fingerprints.

The animal's severed tail was also missing, presumably eaten by the ex-whisperer, who handed himself in to the police at approximately 4.30am, weeping quietly.

33

Another missive in God's unsettling, backward-sloping handwriting has arrived in my mailbox.

"Brad, who can fathom the mind of God?" it begins. "Sometimes it even surprises me.

"For instance, while washing the dishes I find myself thinking about a cormorant. It may be the bird that is foremost in my mind, or it may just be the word. I'm scrubbing a saucepan with wire wool.

"Cormorant is a pretty word, reminding me of 'celebrant' and 'supplicant' and 'cor blimey!' The exemplary phrase 'Cor blimey, the celebrant murdered the supplicant!' brings the image of killer cormorants to mind, dressed in dog collars, perhaps as a disguise to fox the police. I am by now removing brown stains from a tea cup.

"For some reason, the word 'cormorant' also makes me think of the word 'ptarmigan', although there is no connection between them except that they are both birds. Sorry, I mean, rather, that they are both words. And both have nine letters. The proposition 'cormorants often murder ptarmigans' flashes into my head at this point. I am removing butter from the blade of a knife.

"I don't think cormorants really do murder ptarmigans. It's

something I could arrange should I so wish. I could make it an iron-clad law of nature, but the Law of Unintended Consequences might make it do something unpleasant, like flatten Kiev. Let's see, how would that happen? Cormorants wipe out ptarmigans, whose foodstock the Hyrcanian cuttlefish consequently flourishes, battling back the Black Sea sturgeon with which it normally competes for duckweed. Kiev's caviar trade is consequently wiped out, causing builders to skimp on materials, and when the next major storm crosses the wheat fields... Boom! Act of God.

"Anyway, 'ptarmigan', the word not the bird, makes me think of 'pterodactyl' and 'Michigan' and 'tarnish', as in the sentence: 'A pterodactyl flapped into Michigan, tarnished by murder most foul!' At that point I begin thinking about dactylography, which in English is the scientific study of fingerprints, but in French means simply typing. As in 'the murdered French typist exchanged dactylographie for dactylography'. At this moment, I am scrubbing yolk-smear from an egg cup.

"Dostoyevsky says in *Notes From the Underground*: 'Oh, gentlemen, do you know, perhaps I consider myself an intelligent man only because all my life I have been able neither to begin nor to finish anything. Granted I am a babbler, a harmless vexatious babbler, like all of us. But what is to be done if the direct and sole vocation of every intelligent man is babble, that is, the intentional pouring of water through a sieve?'

"I am dabbing a tea towel over my dishes when an Elvis Costello line pops into my head: *She's filing her nails as they drag in the lake*. Listening to that song, I always wondered how she could file her nails underwater. Then suddenly I realise that 'they' doesn't refer to her nails, but to policemen.

"But how is she managing to file policemen underwater? If you have any ideas, Brad, please do write back."

34

It's mid-Thargelion. *Anemondoides* (root grumous, flower umbellate, lobes palmate) progresses on long footsalks. I'm walking towards the sporting warehouse when I hear the clopping of horses' hooves on the road behind me.

"Hail, friend! Well met!"

I recognise the voice of Karl Heinrich, the German business-man. He's riding a trap drawn by an enormous shaggy-fetlocked carthorse. His face is covered in a black beekeeper's cloche with a white band.

"Karl! What are you doing here? I thought you'd be back in Germany by now!"

"I decided to join the Glandinians and remain in your country", smiles Karl, opening the veil to reveal a grinning yellow-tanned face.

"The Glandinians?"

"We're a religious community, Brad. We have a little compound just outside Summerville where we try to follow the teachings of our prophet, Henry Hamilton. Hey, I'm heading up there now, why don't you hop up and come visit with us?"

I'm about to shake my head when a giddy sense of possibility stirs within me. Why should I head back into my old life when a new one might be calling me? Besides, Karl's pale blue eyes inspire trust.

As we ride towards Glandinia, Karl begins to tell me how our first meeting was an important spur towards the life he's leading now.

"Brad, you helped me to see that anything is possible if the mind wills it. Do you remember how we floated up to your special place above the atrium?"

"I certainly do. Unfortunately", I tell Karl, "my ability to levitate is strictly confined to the premises at Willy's. It's one reason I was heading there today to try and get my old job back. I miss flapping through the air like a stingray through water."

"Well, I can't promise you that you'll fly in Glandinia, but I can tell you that your soul will grow wings", says Karl. His open-hearted sincerity takes the sheen of cliché off the words. "I'd like you to meet Rainer Gotting, our chief compliance officer."

"Compliance?"

But before Karl can explain, we pull up to a compound fence composed of pointed stakes of charred cedar. At a curt signal from Karl—a decoy birdcall made with fingers and lips—the gate is winched open from inside, and the cart pulls into a central cobbled courtyard.

I'm astonished to see a gleaming branch of Starbucks standing before us.

"Starbucks? That's the last thing I expected to see here!"

"It tends to surprise people who don't know the teachings of our leader, Henry Hamilton. You see, Hamilton believed that heaven could be built right here on earth. What's more, he assured his followers that all the necessary means to achieve perfection already exist in the regulatory structure we have put in place. All that's needed is the full implementation of existing laws and regulations."

"And the Starbucks?"

"Rainer Gotting will explain that. Here, let's go inside!"

The Starbucks is unlike any I've seen. Inside, everything is somehow cleaner and clearer, more precise and pleasing. Unfamiliar but soothing music plays. The coffee smells amazing. I feel as if I've stepped fifty years into the future.

Gotting—reclining on a deck chair in an alcove—is a rugged Viking of a man. He's entirely naked. His penis swings at his waist like an unsheathed scabbard. When Karl rejoins us I'm amazed to see that he's naked too. His physique is tight and tanned. The men signal me to sit down. So far there's no pressure for me to remove my clothes, although I'm already feeling anomalous.

"You ordered a skinny latte, right?" asks Karl. While he's away fetching the drinks, Gotting the Giant explains the Starbucks.

"What we do here is build models of what bits of the world would look like if only they were constructed in full accordance with all applicable laws, by-laws, regulations and conventions. You have to realise, Brad, that most things in this world come about through shabby pacts of happenstance, compromise, blind-eye and baksheesh. The way things are supposed to happen and the way they actually do are completely different."

"Oh, I've had some experience in the retail trade, and I know just what you mean", I concur. Gotting's nudity gives him a moral authority that's difficult to stand up to.

"Our late leader, Henry Hamilton, was a local government enforcer, but despite his best efforts at making organisations fully compliant with all the binding rules and regulations, even he had to admit that what happens, in the best possible circumstances, is what we'd have to call 'selective application'. Some rules are insisted upon, others ignored. And this makes a mockery of the whole legislative apparatus."

"I can see that", I say. "But why build a Starbucks in your back yard?"

"Brad", says Gotting, leaning forward and touching my knee, "this is not just any Starbucks. It's a utopian Starbucks. The Starbucks of Things-As-They-Ought-To-Be. It's how a Starbucks would be in a world in which every applicable rule and regulation were followed."

"And just taste the coffee!" says Karl, handing me my paper cup.

It certainly is an extraordinary taste. One sip and I seem to experience weightlessness and hear the stabbing and ebbing resonance of a thousand xylophones. The clouds dust a sparkle of snow across the summit of Sassafras Mountain, suddenly visible on the horizon through a fanlight window. I take a munch at the macadamia nut biscotti served with my latte.

"That biscotti you just nibbled", observes Gotting. "Have you ever had biscotti in Starbucks before? If so, it was vanilla almond flavour. Right? That's because nowhere else in the world is macadamia nut biscotti served in a Starbucks. And yet a law passed by Congress in 1992, still in force today, stipulates that at least two flavours of biscotti must be available in every branch of Starbucks."

"So why isn't it enforced?" I ask.

"Lobbying", sighs Karl. "Starbucks pays lobbyists millions each year to manipulate politicians in a thousand little ways.

Including, ironically, bribing them with the very biscotti Starbucks is failing to supply."

"Lobbying and special interests have undermined everything. Henry Hamilton saw it all coming. He had the vision to instruct his followers to assemble in places of perfection and shore up against the coming deluge of mediocrity."

"You know", I say, excitedly, "what you're describing is something I was hoping to achieve at Willy's. I know… I know that if I can win Willy's trust, I can make Willy's the best Willy's it could possibly be!"

The two men look gloomy.

"Brad", sighs Karl, "what you have just said is—to us—the ultimate in blasphemy. How to explain?"

Gotting takes over. "By the time he came to write his sacred text *The Manual of Full Compliance*, Henry Hamilton did not believe the world would ever allow itself to be improved, even to the level of its own declared standards. And so worldly improvement, as we call it, has been marked as a sterile and barren pursuit. We believe that full compliance can only be reached in compounds like this one, places apart. All we can do here is make a ghost world, and demonstrate its superiority to all who will listen."

"But if the real world out there is a lost cause, what's the good of that?"

"Don't you see, Brad? We will expand these compounds, and draw more and more people to us. Eventually the superiority of our way of life will become obvious to all. Our new ways will replace their old ones. Our charred cedar fences will expand until they vanish behind every horizon. Our Starbucks will become the real ones, theirs will look like cheap and inferior copies.

"Starbucks is just the beginning", says Gotting, rising to his full height and brandishing his naked penis like a spear. "Soon we will rebuild everything in its ideal version. Everything substandard will be razed to the ground. Full compliance will prevail."

35

The second meeting with Abraham, my son by Agatha Moudio, takes place at the McDonald's in the commercial centre at Old Orangeburg Road. There's a bit of a glitch when the server mistakenly charges my AmEx $22 for two $8 meals and takes twenty-five Miley Cyrus-filled minutes to fix the error. Tempers fray, but Abe and I are eventually sitting face-to-face across a table smelling of apple cinnamon oatmeal and spray bleach.

It shouldn't be surprising, because this is a small town, but it turns out we have quite a few mutual friends in Summerville. Abe knows Bernard Herrmann's brother Albrecht, for instance. He's also learning Indian classical scales out at the pizza restaurant with Pranay, Ritesh, Vimal and Anish. And at weekends God gives him free milkshakes at Tastee Freez.

It soon becomes clear that God is using Abraham to send me messages. It was God who hooked us up, after all. The janitordivinity wants me to get back to the Wonder Voyage mission. He's apparently a bit dismayed that, one year on, I haven't advanced at all. It does look bad, I have to admit. I really need to get my act together.

I try to change the subject. "Is that a Salt Life hoodie?"

It is. In fact, Abraham knows the Four Watermen too. He starts insinuating that they'd be a great crew for my sea voyage.

"I've screened the Watermen. They would make a lousy crew. Anyway, I hear that one of them has died."

"That still leaves three."

He's a pushy kid. Reminds me of me.

"What do you want? You want your old Dad to drown at sea because three ancient elves didn't know their leech tension from their boom vangs?"

"Elves know more than you give them credit for, Dad."

136

36

It is the month of Skirophorion. The American hornbeam, acrid fugitive of the oaklands bordering the Santee swamps near Laneau's Ferry, emits a sinister rustle.

Brad has finally been able to mount the Wonder Voyage to uninvent America.

After fasting for forty days and doing hard penance, he has constructed a very large ship with strong hides nailed over it, and pitch over the hides, so that the water can't come in.

The twelve members of the crew accompanying him in the leather coracle are the three remaining Avid Watermen, Ralf Hutter from Kraftwerk, Hulk Hogan, Dusty Hill from ZZ Top, Preciosa Mendoza and her globular sister Dolorosa, shamanic animal consultant Chuck Atkins, Jan Lindenberg and his "dog" Peter Saville, and Brad's son Abraham.

Now, on paper this may not sound like the ideal team to pack together in a small sea vessel. The paper-thin Watermen are in their eighties, Kraftwerk and ZZ Top still hate each other, Preciosa has no nautical experience, and her sister Dolorosa is severely disabled. As for Chuck Atkins, he's the most annoying man ever. But dressed in identical yellow sou'westers, they certainly look like a team as they step off the Charleston jetty into the coracle, singing in one voice:

Row, fisherman, row
Keep on rowing your boat!
Lots of hungry-belly pickney they ashore
Millions of them!

Seated in the leather-bottom vessel, the crew tell Brad that they have left their friends and all their goods of their own free will, and have come as children to him, and that whatever he thinks well to do, they will do it.

And Brad takes the twelve with him, and bids farewell to South Carolina. They row out into the great sea of the ocean in the name of our Lord and are in no way daunted at all. And the sea and the wind drive the ship at will, so that on the morning of the following day they are out of sight of land. And so they continue through forty days, with the wind driving them eastward.

And the coracle is called the *UnAmerica*.

37

There are things a landman cannot know. This is the knowledge of the waterman. It snows from the north. The earth is a page without writing. Salt is on our tongues. Snow is the coldest of grains.

Not for us the sound of the harp, nor the giving of matrimonial rings! No pleasure for us, or glory! We shall eat only fish, and the bones of fish shall catch in our throats.

Soon all will become cold and white. The sea will be white, the sky white, the day white and the night white. White birds will follow the white boat with jeering cries.

Little by little we will each forget food, and sex, and even sleep. We will leave the land of America far behind, and the fair town, and the field rich with blossoms and harvests, and the lingonberry in season.

Out on the freezing sea the day will be white and the night, too. Metal with cold will grow our white feet, clamped in irons of frost. We will have no clansmen except each other, and for song only the screech of the white gannet and gull, and for orchestra only the howling of the wind.

We shall row all mute. The icebergs shall float by, horrible, like geographical screams. We will see a ghastly white whale, or think we do. Our craft will heave and lurch, in the grip of grimmest storm. We shall fear doom by wrecking and death by drowning.

It is longing that shall sting us along. Longing for the God who has sent us on this Wonder Voyage, and lust for the lands beyond.

White, white, white! On the coracle we will not even sing. The whole earth will be a page of harsh, blank ocean water.

Suddenly:

"Abaft the fore hatch!" the Matelot will call.

"Oilskins on for outhaul!" will issue from the Packetman.

"Man the yards!" the Midshipman will roar.

"Swing the mizzenmast!" the Old Man will concur.

"Mind the beakhead!" the Anchor Watch will warn.

"Scupper the gaff vang and gird up the futtocks!" will thunder Grunt.

"Parbuckle the scantlings!" McWhirter will ejaculate, thickly.

"Genoa the schreecher!" will echo the Third Mate.

"Razzee all drabblers on the quarterdeck!" the Landlubber will shriek.

"Gooseneck the gin pole!" the Hawsepiper will shrill.

"Lock down the jigger-mast!" will sing Jolly Jack Tar.

"Purge the lazaret!" will thunder Loggerhead Bill.

"Land ahoy!" will shrill the Barrelman.

And we shall beach on the first island, a place of low compounds outside of which will stand knots of men and women smoking passive-aggressively.

It shall do our hearts right good to be on land again!

As we crunch up the shingle, talk will turn to verbs.

"The English language is a prowless skiff", McWhirter observera, "for it sorely lacks a decent future tense. If I were to report as a thing in the future this event we are now living out, for example, I would soon tire of saying will this and shall that, as English requires me to do."

"Aye", Jack Tar assentera, "English-speaking men and women have but scant care for events in the future. 'Tis not the cut of their jib to think on future things, for the scurvy dogs are a backward-looking race."

"The French", the Matelot repondra, "now that's a people that respects the future!"

"I reckon", suggerera Loggerhead Bill, "that this is something people of the Anglosphere will one day demand of their political class: a decent future tense for English."

"To hell with the political class", spittera Grunt. "The people themselves agiront!"

The crew of the *UnAmerica* will arrive at a cluster of compounds of indeterminate purpose. If they are supermarkets, they will be surprised to find that fruit and vegetables are less expensive than meat and that they will be expected to pay in cash. They will not be required to tip the man who carries the groceries back to the coracle for them: "I'm paid for this by the store!" he'll explain cheerfully.

The chocolate they will buy will be surprisingly tasty, the Kit-

Kat oil-free. The dessert section will be very small. Turkey will not be on sale. There will be no two-for-one offers.

If, on the other hand, the white compounds be hospitals, the crew of the *UnAmerica* shall not be asked, immediately on entering: "Now, how do you intend to pay for this?"

If the white compounds be banks, and they make a transfer between one and the other, no paper checks will be issued at any point. The transfer will be entirely electronic.

If the white compounds be military bases, they will not be surveying the private communications of citizens all over the world, nor planning drone strikes against civilians in far-off lands.

If the white compounds be branches of Starbucks and McDonald's, the coffee and hamburgers will be of surprisingly good quality.

However, the crew of the *UnAmerica* will soon discover that the white compounds are none of these things: they are all branches of IKEA.

38

O to be in Sweden! For Sweden rhymes with freedom. How correctly did Osama observe: "Had I hated freedom, I would have attacked Sweden!"

When a man is in IKEA, he is always in Sweden, wherever he really is. And when a man is in his IKEA-furnished house, his house is in Sweden, wherever it may really stand. Increasingly, we are living in "a Sweden of the mind". And we are better for it.

The crew of the *UnAmerica* will make straight for the furniture section. The Matelot and the Packetman will sink into the KLIPPAN loveseat, an item of furniture too sexual ever to have been conceived by an American mind. The Midshipman and the Old Man will sit side-by-side in two olive green NOLMYRA easy chairs, lightweight and easy to lift out of the way to make room for play.

Preciosa Mendosa and her ball-like sister Dolorosa (known on the coracle as Anchor Watch and Grunt) will strip off and roll naked in TEJN, a faux-sheepskin rug priced at just $9.99. McWhirter, the Third Mate and the Landlubber will sit like a row of identical gnomes on the green STOCKHOLM sofa, whose cushions mould to the contours of your body and then puff back into shape when you leave.

The Hawsepiper and Jolly Jack Tar will recline on the liberalising upholstery of FRIHETEN, the new hot pink corner bed which radicalises traditional conceptions of horizontality and verticality. Meanwhile Loggerhead Bill and the Barrelman will be making messy love on SÖDERHAMN, the modular seating combination that seats you and thirteen of your favourite people.

Later, dining on meatballs liberally dowsed with lingonberry sauce, the crew of the *UnAmerica* will feel deeply happy.

"One day", Grunt will muse, "the whole world will be Sweden."

"Yes, one day the whole world will be Sweden!" It will be an old man's voice, with a Swedish accent. The thirteen members of the *UnAmerica* crew will swivel on their BOJNE chairs, made of pale beech, to see none other than Ingvar Kamprad before them.

IKEA's founder and owner will be wearing a purple leisure suit with a round-lapelled, double-breasted jacket and jodhpurs tucked into thigh-high patent leather jackboots. He will stand just one meter tall. "Furniture is only a means to an end", he will tell them.

"All nations and societies in both the East and West spend a disproportionate amount of their resources on satisfying a minority of the population", IKEA's leader will say in a speech delivered tomorrow in the IKEA cafe. "In our line of business, for example, far too many of the fine designs and new ideas are reserved for a small circle of the affluent. We have decided once and for all to side with the many.

"We aim to be simple and straightforward in ourselves and in our dealings with others", the Swede—whose complicated corporate structure culminates in a series of tax-avoiding charity organisations and holding companies registered in the Netherlands, Luxembourg and Lichtenstein—will confess. "The ultimate goal, however, is to control the way life is lived everywhere. That is why it is our duty to expand.

"Politicians have merely made laws which can only be enforced by the police", Kamprad—whose company name is composed of his initials and those of the Swedish farm and village he grew up in (Ingvar Kamprad Elmtaryd Agunnaryd)—will continue. "But the point is to change the daily routines of life by getting inside the needs and desires of ordinary people. Who needs police when your furniture is telling you how to live?

"Think of ancient Egypt", Kamprad, who is almost ninety and unimaginably rich, will tell the crew of the *UnAmerica*. "Do we know about them because of the laws they followed? Certainly not. We know their death artefacts, and the para-phernalia of their daily lives. When I die I will leave more ethnographic treasures for future archeologists than all the pharaohs put together!"

And with that the world's most powerful man—who drives an old Volvo, travels economy class on airlines, was unfortunately a member of a fascist-nationalist party in his youth, wrote a book called *The Testament of a Furniture Dealer*, names his chairs after small towns in Finland and releases a catalogue which is more popular than the Bible—will disappear into his store's labyrinthine one-way system in an electrically-powered golf cart.

When we have reprovisioned the coracle with vasterbottensost, tarta blabar, godis skruvblandning, knackebrod rag and saft fläder, we shall leave the first island.

39

Many will wonder—and often—how the seafarer can consider the constantly-churning waters of the sea any sort of home. Hardship is an endless curse. As the seafarer heaves and retches on his bobbing cork, the rowing seems to rip the very arms from his shoulders. The shadows deepen at dusk, and the ocean deepens, too. Soon fear and boredom descend, his only feal bondsmen. Sometimes in the keening wind the seafarer hears the screams of the drowned, deep in their darkened lair.

The city man, red-faced with wine and chomping on pork, must find it hard to fathom, like a pig dazzled by a beach ball. But the sea will prove its rewards to the brave. If you continue to haul your slow coracle across the fizzing scurf for three days, aiming your prow away from America, you will reach a second island.

"Land ahoy!" will thunder Loggerhead Bill.

"Avast the belay!" the Matelot will call.

"Hold helm to leeward!" will issue from the Packetman.

"Jury rig the gammon iron!" the Midshipman will roar.

"Ram the joggle!" the Old Man will concur.

"The scantlings are unspliced!" the Anchor Watch will warn.

"Knockdown the Midshipman's nuts!" will thunder Grunt.

"Jibe ho on handy billy!" McWhirter will ejaculate, thickly.

"Tar-foul the range!" will echo the Third Mate.

"Luff up the Inglefield clip!" the Landlubber will shriek.

"Hull down the lugger!" the Hawsepiper will shrill.

"Devil seam the foulies!" will trill Jolly Jack Tar.

"Hornpipe up the footrope!" will shrill the Barrelman.

And the entire crew will nimbly hornpipe up the footrope.

The second island will be peaceful, fruitful, temperate. Persimmon trees will stud small leafy hills with spots of vivid dark orange. At the top of the central mound will stand an art-house cinema. A carefully-designed noticeboard will announce three films:

Voyage on the North Sea by Marcel Broodthaers (1974, 6 mins)
Volcano Saga by Joan Jonas (1985, 28 mins)
A Journey That Wasn't by Pierre Huyghe (2005, 25 mins)

The crew will file into the darkened room and take their seats in surprisingly comfort. The Broodthaers film will not be well received, however.

"It's a bit slow!" the Matelot will whisper.

"It's nothing but still photographs of boats!" will sneer the Packetman.

"My son could do that!" the Midshipman will mutter.

"I've seen it on YouTube!" the Old Man will sigh.

"There's fluff in the gate!" the Anchor Watch will scoff.

"That's not fluff, it's pubes!" will thunder Grunt.

The entire crew will laugh raucously.

"What's the projectionist up to?" McWhirter will ejaculate, thickly.

"Better not ask!" will titter the Third Mate.

"Well, he's having more fun than we are!" the Landlubber will shriek.

"This is boring!" the Hawsepiper will shrill.

"Look, a close-up of paint drying!" will trill Jolly Jack Tar.

"Look out, the sea's drying up!" will shrill the Barrelman.

"Next!" will thunder Loggerhead Bill.

And as if on cue, the next presentation will begin. Now a rapt hush will descend on the men and women in the audience.

Tilda Swinton is playing Gudrun, the most beautiful woman in 13th-century Iceland, and no less clever than she is good-looking. Gudrun asks a wise kinsman to interpret four dreams she's had, all involving rings. As they steep in bubbling hot water, the kinsman interprets the dreams: they're premonitions of betrothals and marriages. Gudrun's four husbands will all die. The tales, accompanied by Quantel Paintbox and green-screen images of sheep, moss, fish, birds, seals and the sulphuric mists and jagged mountain masses of Iceland, are drawn from the *Laxdæla* saga.

The crew of the *UnAmerica* will be spellbound and speechless when the Jonas video is over. The women will think of their own husbands, and the men of their wives, imaginary or real.

But already the next film is beginning. A voice-over announces that a tragic odyssey is being mounted in a splendid schooner. The destination is an uncharted island in the Antarctic, newly uncovered by the receding ice. There are seven artists and ten crew members on board. Their mission is to find and film a legendary solitary albino penguin.

The vessel sets sail from Tierra del Fuego. The schooner bashes its way through icy waters, a huge storm engulfs it, then the sea is once more becalmed. Companionable whales and dolphins surface and dive, gulls caw and circle, fish are caught, the schooner gets locked in the ice then breaks free, enormous waves tilt and swell. At last the island is glimpsed, a landing is made, and a research station is set up containing delicate experimental equipment designed to facilitate communication with the mythical creature.

Yellow-hatted figures in orange boiler suits, sharp as persimmons against the snow, erect balloon-shaped arc-lights like the ones used on Japanese construction sites. Microphones are placed on stands; they will collect information about the shape of the island using sound alone. As darkness falls the lights shine like mysterious white planets, attracting curious penguins. The information gathered is translated into a series of mechanical cries designed to attract the albino penguin.

At last the flightless white bird, almost invisible against its white background, waddles up. The entire cinema breaks into applause.

"Hurrah!" the Matelot will whisper.

"I do like a happy ending!" will sniffle the Packetman.

"Well done, those artists!" the Midshipman will mutter.

"That albino is a fine specimen!" the Old Man will sigh.

"The only one of its kind!" the Anchor Watch will concur.

"A miracle!" will thunder Grunt.

"Would that all odysseys were so 'tragic'!" McWhirter will ejaculate, thickly.

"I wept!" the Third Mate will confess.

"Me too!" the Landlubber will shriek.

"An afternoon well spent!" the Hawsepiper will gloat.

"I feel ready to continue!" will trill Jolly Jack Tar.

"Yes, my resolve is now doubled!" will shrill the Barrelman.

"Onward!" will thunder Loggerhead Bill.

And so, hauling hundreds of hurriedly-picked persimmons in plastic bags, the crew will return to the *UnAmerica*.

40

Our heroes will sail a long time on the sea before they next see any land. It will be a very green island, and when they land and look about them they will see sheep on every side, the whitest and the finest that ever were seen, for every sheep will be the size of an ox. Then there will come to them an elegant old man who will welcome them kindly, saying: "This place you have come to is the Land of Sheep, and there is never winter here but lasting summer, and that is why the sheep are so large and so white, for the grass and the herbs are the best to be found in any place at all. And go on", he will tell them, "until you come by the grace of God to a place that is called the Paradise of Birds; and it is there you will keep your Easter."

But, setting out again, the coracle will quickly run into difficulties due to sudden appalling weather conditions. They will eventually founder on a submerged reef not far from the Paradise of Birds. But because conditions are so bad, they will be forced to remain on board, and hope that the craft can be refloated at high tide.

Throughout the day they will see an enormous seal swimming in the current, circling the boat. It will have huge flippers, and everyone will think its eyes are those of a human. Brad—the Old Man—will tell his crew to harpoon the seal. After many failed attempts, the Hawsepiper—Ralf Hutter from Kraftwerk—will score a direct hit through one of the animal's blue eyes. Blood will stain the entire bay red, and the seal's hulking corpse will be so huge it will form a land bridge from the reef to the island. One by one the crew of the *UnAmerica* will cross this bridge, bouncing on the seal's still-warm blubber.

On the shore will stand a woman, big and angry-looking. "Are you asleep?" she will ask Brad the Old Man.

"No, I am awake", he will reply.

"You are asleep, but that makes no difference", the woman will say. "You have killed my son and returned him to me mutilated."

And with that the woman will vanish.

The crew of the *UnAmerica* will be hungry now, having exhausted their supplies of IKEA food. Brad the Old Man will instruct them to chop hunks of seal blubber out of the land bridge. They will set up a cauldron on the beach and light a fire to boil it. No sooner will the fire grow hot and the blubber begin to boil than the island will start to quake and move like a living thing. There will be great fear amongst the crew.

Skipping precariously over the disintegrating land bridge, squelchy with blood, all thirteen will hasten back to the coracle, leaving the food and the cauldron behind them. From the *UnAmerica* they will see with astonishment what they took to be an island moving quickly through the sea, a fire burning on its back.

Brad the Old Man will enlighten them: "It is a great seal, the biggest in the world. Her name is Jasconye, and day and night she is trying to put her tail into her mouth, but she cannot do it because of her great bulk. She believed her son Harry would help her, but we killed him. Now she is angry with us and will seek our destruction if she sees us again."

The crew of the *UnAmerica* will be deathly afraid when they hear this, and will row away from that place with great haste.

41

Suddenly a cloud will gather around them, and they will be in darkness the whole of the day, until by the will of our dear Lord the cloud shall pass and disperse, and they will see before them a shining lovely continent, and that will be called Eurasia.

There will be much joy and rejoicing in that landmass, where every herb will be full of blossom and every tree full of fruit; and as for the ground it will be shining with precious stones on every side, and heaven itself could hardly be better.

Then there will come to them a very comely young man that will know every one of them by name and give them a pleasant welcome:

Welcome, the Matelot, also known as spirit-animal consultant Chuck Atkins!

Welcome, the Packetman, also known as Jan Lindenberg!

Welcome, the Midshipman, also known as Abraham, son of Brad!

Welcome, the Anchor Watch, also known as Preciosa Mendoza!

Welcome, Grunt, her rotund sister Dolorosa Mendoza!

Welcome, McWhirter, the so-called "dog" Peter Saville!

Welcome, the Third Mate, or the first avid waterman!

Welcome, the Hawsepiper, also known as Ralf Hutter!

Welcome, the Landlubber, the second avid waterman!

Welcome, the Barrelman, Hulk Hogan!

Welcome, Jolly Jack Tar, the third avid waterman!

Welcome, Loggerhead Bill, Dusty Hill from ZZ Top!

And welcome Brad Power, the Old Man, captain of this voyage, dearly beloved of God, and soon to be known as Saint Brad!

"It would be right for you to give good thanks to me", Jesus Christ will say, "for this is the continent I will give to my darlings upon earth at the world's end, and it is to this place I myself will come.

"And", Jesus will continue, "there is another island besides this one, but you have not leave to go on to it or to have sight of it at all."

It will transpire that the crew of the *UnAmerica* will have been in that continent for six months without meat or drink or sleep, although it will only have felt like half an hour, so happy and content will they be there. And apparently—according to the comely young man, Jesus Christ—that place was the first dwelling place of Adam and Eve, and darkness never comes there, and the name of the place is Eurasia, or the Earthly Paradise.

Then the comely man—who looks like a young version of the janitor at Tastee Freez—will bring them back to their ship again, and, when they're safe on board, will vanish.

42

Now our heroes, led by Saint Brad, will set out across the sea again, and where they come to land they will tell the people that they have been to the gates of Paradise, in the Land of Promise called Eurasia, and had every sort of joy there and of feasting, and that there is always day in that place and no night at all.

And their clothes will have the sweetness of that place still lingering about them, and the people will say: "We are certain indeed you have been in that Eurasian paradise, by the happy smiles on you all!"

And God will bless the crew of the *UnAmerica*, and say unto them: "Be fruitful, and multiply, and replenish the earth, and subdue it, and have dominion over the fish of the sea, and over the fowl of the air, and over every living thing that moveth upon the earth!"

And at that the men will look with some ambivalence at the women, Grunt and the Anchor Watch.

And God will continue, "I think my memory is coming back. I think I know now why I couldn't create anything. It wasn't because of Alzheimers. It was because I had forgotten how to forget, and how to destroy."

"Saint Brad", God will say, "with this voyage you have reminded me how forgetting is done. Be fruitful, Old Man, and multiply, and fill the waters in the seas, and let fowl multiply in the earth!"

And again the men will look with some ambivalence at Grunt and the Anchor Watch, and wish that God had given them some more appealing women.

And God will lean back, incredibly cool and in his element, and create great whales, and every living creature that moveth, which the waters bring forth abundantly, after their kind, and every winged fowl after its kind: and God will see that it is bloody good.

And God will say: "These creatures were endangered, but now they are going to be plentiful again. And now let the waters bring forth abundantly the moving creatures that hath life, and fowl that may fly above the earth in the open firmament of heaven."

And God will remember he's forgetting something, and will set two great lights in the firmament of the heaven to give light upon the earth, and to rule over the day and over the night, and to divide the light from the darkness. And God will make the stars also, not necessarily as an afterthought, but just to prove he's good, and it will be so.

And the earth will bring forth grass, and herb yielding seed after its kind, and the tree yielding fruit, whose seed is in itself, after its kind: and God will see just how extremely excellent it all is.

And God will now be on a roll, and will say: "Let the earth bring forth grass, the herb yielding seed, and the fruit tree yielding fruit after its kind, whose seed is in itself, upon the earth." And it will jolly well be so.

And God will call the dry land Earth. And the gathering together of the waters will call he Seas. And God will smile, for this is a vastly better job than being a janitor at Tastee Freez.

And God will say: "Let the waters under the heaven be gathered together unto one place, and let the dry land appear." And presto, it will be so!

And God will call the land Eurasia, Africa and Australia, and the firmament Heaven.

And God will say: "Let there be light!" And there, rising in the East, will be light.

And in the West, America will be without form, and void. And darkness will be upon the face of that place.

And finally it will be just as if America had never existed.

And the Spirit of God will move upon the face of the waters.

Success and Failure Series

 PENNY-ANTE | EDITIONS
PO BOX 691578 LOS ANGELES CA 90069
UNITED STATES OF AMERICA